FEN ROADS

JENI NEILL

FEN TIGER PRESS

PUBLISHED BY:

Fen Tiger Press

ISBN: 978-1-8381492-2-2
eBook IBSN: 978-1-8381492-3-9

For all the colours you are,

And all that you bring…

For Marcus

Blending

I didn't make that hair, it's not from me;
The curls that people love to pat and comment on as
quite a head.
I wash and cut and put on the gel that defines and
softens each dark tress.
I am the keeper of the hair.

I don't own the dancing gene, the gifted prance flying
with electric charge,
Leaving rainbow twirls and sparks of life; making
smiles and turning heads.
I encourage, take to classes, pay the fees.
I am the watcher of the skill.

I can't talk about your birth, the time it took to lift
you into the world.
That journeys lost in paths unknown, as are those
ineffable newborn days.
I link stories to photos and share what we know.
I am your past's guardian, nothing more.

Some parts of you remain opaque still, erupting in
storm and ill blown wind.
Behaviour to be decoded, explored, managed,
tolerated…patience. Patience.
But love's settled here, not presumed and never
owned.
I am the mother of that love.

— JENI NEILL 2015

FOREWORD

When I was young, maybe ten, there was nothing l liked
more than to lay belly down on the floor creating families
in my head. I'd draw each figure to then cut out as a paper
person. I created scenery from sheets of folded paper,
which would be the rooms in their homes or their outside
yards. I would know how each character interconnected
with their neighbour and within their extended families.
The stories would build and build, becoming quite
involved and exacting. Names and ages were written on the
back of each person and there were always plenty of dogs.

Now, as I have enjoyed writing this collection of short
stories, I see that this process has been very similar to that
past recollection. I now form the scenes in written form,
rather than my vulnerable thin-papered alternative, and I
smile to think that these families and their circumstances
have always lived within me. They are very much part of
who I am. As are The Fens.

The first few stories have tenuous links to the Fens, as I feel
they serve as a journey into that area. As the stories take
you further in, to the links and situations, The Fens become

much more integral to the subsequent tales. For this reason, the stories are probably best read in sequence. But these stories are not only about the Fens. They touch on what it means to connect with other people, to belong, and what is needed to flourish; rather like the soil itself.

The book's cover is a painting by my father called Fen Road. He painted this when I was two years old, and it most likely hung on a wall in each of the houses we lived in. I hated it. It was everything I wanted to move away from. My father was fascinated by the landscape, it crept into most everything he ever seemed to paint. Norfolk is his family's bloodline, through and through, without interruption.

Being born in Wisbech, and to parents who didn't drive, the feeling of being held by the landscape and not being able to escape it was intense. The colour and unknown fragrance of exotic faraway lands, which spanned from as far as the West Indies (in books) to Hunstanton (in reality) left an impression. But it was my everyday surroundings that later inspired me; the ever stretching, muddy riverbanks and roads that seemed to be not worth the travel, in their bleak promise of nothing but the same. I just didn't appreciate the benefits of this rather suffocating affect at the time. Like my father's artwork, it was just a reminder of the flat and horizontal lines that I pleaded with internally to explode and reform; to rearrange as a dramatically different picture.

I hope any Fen people who read my stories will see my learned regard and respect for it, as well as my understanding of its harsh outlines and foreboding presence. I realise that not everyone feels this as intensely and some are, like my father, left uplifted by its span and seemingly minimal terrain. But, for me, it is the most demanding landscape I have ever encountered; it has knocked at my soul and battered for gratification, as if a dark and threatening wave were repeatedly held over me. Its presence has walked where I walk, whether out of Fen or within it. Its people, my people, have left their mark.

I have avoided using known Fen surnames, and so the ones used may stem from far and wide of the area. All my characters are fictional but are often influenced by those we meet along the way. Sometimes, these are people who are just overheard and never known, while others are very familiar, maybe leaving injuries that can be moulded to a kinder form within the written word, or having made a positive impact on an impressionable mind. My connection to the children in Care comes through love of one of my own, and all the lessons we learn together as our own back stories blend.

At the end of my collection, I have placed a Character Tree to show how the stories' characters intertwine. This may have been quite apparent anyway but it's fun to do, so please excuse my indulgence. Like my paper people days, I can invent their imaginary connections and this, once again, has been a favourite part of my creating this book. I hope you enjoy it. If you do, I'd love to hear from you. Maybe, you could let me know which was your favourite story, if you leave an online review.

SHARP AS SHARPE

'Not a crumb in sight,' Betty proudly boasts, having patted her lips with her precisely folded napkin. Arnold, her caged parrot, repeats 'no crumb' as he has every morning, at this time, for the last fourteen years; just as, at nine-thirty every evening, he copies 'lights out'.

At six-thirty, breakfast eaten, spick and span, Betty Sharpe clicks her fingers restlessly. Lockdown has her off work and increasingly bored. Never having reduced her hours in preparation for her imminent retirement, this lack of structure and routine has been as unwelcome as any derailment could possibly be.

Betty raises her eyes to the plop of the newspaper pushed through her letterbox. This particular newspaper boy pleases her with his time-keeping and the care he takes to actually post the paper completely through the narrow slit. She knows the number of steps she will take to reach it and her snappy scoop to retrieve is worthy of a younger body. But, on briskly opening the closed fold, her eyes stare in horror at the headline that greets her.

'All single households to take in a Homeless!' Her eyes smart with the pressure pushed into their bulge, 'This bloody pandemic! I've had enough of hearing about this ridiculous proposal; having to hear this nonsense for the last two weeks.'

As she continues her rageful grumble she throws the paper to the floor in disgust, as if by doing this the matter will cease to exist, 'Bumbling bloody government. It will amount to no more than another annoying threat,' she reassures herself, looking at her reflection in the antique hall mirror, and grimacing as if at the Prime Minister himself.

Picking the 'dealt with' newspaper up once more, her thoughts are interrupted most unexpectedly by her land-line ringing. It sounds misplaced, remote, and she feels her skin prickle. Like a foghorn in the night. Alien and spooky, as if calling in the ghosts. No one phones me before nine, she reflects, as she snatches the receiver in bewilderment, 'Felixstowe 359201'.

She swiftly interrupts the well-read introduction from the dull voice on the receiver,

'Who are you? Do you think this is amusing?' is all her flabbergasted mind can form in response to his announce-ment, 'As if your department is even open now. I'm not a dithering fool.'

'I'm not at all amused myself, Miss Sharpe, I assure you. We work round the clock currently; our hours aren't what they were. As if Social Services wasn't already over-run with situations,' the tired male voice continues, mostly to himself, 'But we have been instructed to arrange, with immediate effect, to rehome the homeless in known single households.'

'How do you know I live alone?' her tone giving away her total panic, 'I have a parrot. He talks.'

'We know from the Voting Register. Now please try to accept what I am telling you. This isn't easy for anyone.'

'How on earth will this help preserve the NHS? I'm a very important part of the system…vital in fact. I cannot afford to catch Corona from a vagrant!'

'But you're not currently going into work are you, Miss Sharpe? The School of Nursing is shut. I shall bring your Chloe Brown over at 2 p.m.'

'This is outrageous!' Betty Sharpe's foundations wobble for the first time in years. She feels her footing's slide and grabs with her words, 'After ALL I have done for my country, following every rule and expectation that was ever set. Now, in a few weeks of well-earned rest, I…'

'I am sorry to interrupt you, but I have a lot of calls to get through. If you have questions, you can ask me when I come at 2 p.m.'

Betty doesn't know which sting to address first, the slaps of 'your Chloe Brown' or the call being finished abruptly by someone other than her. She storms into her sitting room and stares hard at her reflection in the French door glass, as if to be sure she's not lost in a disgraceful nightmare. Bouncing back with sharp lines from the still dark garden, it gives no comfort. As if to ground herself and deny any deviation, she walks from sofa to sideboard, lamp to picture frame, touching each thing, feeling its reality. The chenille throw, so carefully set on the back of her armchair, is soft yet tightly woven; the mantelpiece, above the gas fire, smooth and dust-free.

She strains at her memory of the call to pick out the girl's name. She has always been good with names, after decades of practice with the quarterly recruitment of student nurses. 'Chloe Brown' hits her hard.

'What sort of a girl gets herself homeless!' she barks in disgust. Raising her nose automatically, as if the atmosphere now contains the most repugnant of smells. 'I am seriously to entertain a tramp in my house? The home of my parents! Oh my God…How they would turn in their graves!'

With the movement of a well-oiled machine, she steers through to the kitchen where she produces a steel glare, enough to strip feathers, as she turns to the African Grey,

'Crumbs!' she spits.

⁂

BETTY WALKS the social worker to exit by her front door, leaving Chloe Brown perched nervously on her sofa. The pandemic rules have all of them donning a mask and observing two-metre distancing, although in her narrow hall it's not possible and Betty's efforts to stretch past the man's sizeable beer belly to open the door snib become almost farcical.

'Promise me this will be for no more than a few weeks. I must have some rights!' Her embarrassment at almost falling onto him make her words all the more brutal.

'I know no more than you, Ms…er…Sharpe.' The weariness in his voice reflected in his lethargic physical movements and lack of expression, 'No one knows how long Lockdown will go on.' As he turns to leave, he looks back at the skeletal woman, 'Go easy on her, will you? She's only a kid.'

'A kid! When I was that age...!' Betty grimaces as she throws the door after him.

Returning to her sitting room, and the now intimate presence of Chloe, she senses fear prickle up her neck; could this be a red rash she feels groping her skin to expose her vulnerability? She attempts to squash it under a scramble of angry words,

'I can't see this working. Maybe, if you keep out of my way, to the room I show you, perhaps we'll get through a few hours of it.'

'Thank you,' the girl replies timidly, wiping her sweaty palms on her well-worn jeans and trying to offer a smile, 'I appreciate what you are doing for me. I've been scared on the street.' Her words are rather muffled by the paper mask covering her mouth, but her pronunciation is careful and considered. This, in itself, augments Betty's spite. For some reason it would be easier if this girl seemed less able.

'I'd ask you why you chose to live that way, but I wouldn't want you to think I care!' Betty spits each word, unable to backtrack her attitude or show any remorse. She appears a little like a tormented cat, back arched and fur upended; so cornered by the position she finds herself in.

'It's not always a choice. Life takes funny turns. It's complicated isn't it.'

Feeling further challenged by the girl's psychology, and baffled by her gentle soft voice and careful reflections, Betty tramples these too, to ensure her own superiority,

'You better get a bath first. I'll have no lice in here. Don't run it deep though; I want hot left.'

5

Noticing Chloe's eyes dazzle, Betty prods the black bin liner roughly with her foot, 'What could you possibly have to feel happy about? Is this all you have?'

'It's just the thought of a bath! That was always a favourite of mine. Well, that and my bed.'

'But the pull of the concrete street was just too much for you! I can imagine the dirty things you got up to in your bed. I will have none of that in here.' Betty clutches her heart dramatically as she imagines what her parents would have said and the dark, devious tricks that this Chloe will no doubt try and get away with. She makes a mental note to hide all window keys; she could wake in the small hours to a party of homeless folk in her very own front room.

Chloe blushes and is relieved to be shown to the privacy of the tired bathroom. She peeks round the door to see the spare-room that Betty is indicating she should use, and just manages to catch the lavender towel thrown for her use. The small, bleak room has no hint of personality and well-stacked boxes are against the wall, leaving only space for the rather functional single bed, wardrobe, and chest of drawers.

'These boxes are full of memorabilia, which I've just gone through rather luckily. You'll have to help me move them into the loft tomorrow. And talking of jobs…' Betty throws spitefully over her shoulder, 'you needn't think I haven't got one. Just because I may look near to retirement, I'm still a very necessary part of society. You and I have nothing in common.'

Chloe can hear Betty banging about, as she slips into the water's luxury. The risky steal of Radox bubbles seems worth taking, as she lowers her whole head into the hot, hugging water.

'I DIDN'T EXPECT to see you up before lunch. It's 6.30am! What kind of a tramp are you?'

Chloe's reticent to enter the kitchen and hovers at the door but her tummy is rumbling and feels as if it's digesting itself, 'Is it alright to get something to eat? I'm so hungry.'

'You could have eaten tea. I told you where it was.'

'I was too nervous to eat last night,' Chloe confesses as she pours some cereal into a delicate china bowl. The All-bran reminds her of shredded cardboard but, quite literally, she knows beggars can't be choosers.

'Don't make crumbs. I keep my house tidy! And don't harden your face to me, young lady.'

"No Crumbs,' says Arnold, hanging upside down.

Betty has the atmosphere in the room coiled tight but Chloe walks to Arnold and speaks softly, bringing her finger tentatively to the cage, 'Is he an African Grey?'

With a display of boredom or weariness, Betty steals any brightness in her story by filling it only with complaint,

'I have no care for him. He belonged to my parents. I always felt he was like a spy, repeating what he'd over-heard. Watching everything with his beady, mean eyes.'

'How old do you think he is?' Chloe persists, determined to break through the woman's frozen barriers.

'He's well over forty. My parents got him when I left for nurse training. Thought I'd gone for good, so replaced me with a parrot! How's that for being valued? But they got me back a few years later: when I was summoned, I returned. My father needed a housekeeper once my

7

mother died. I have always done my duty.' Betty emphasizes each word, as if to grind something unpleasant underfoot, and is so scant with the details it paints a very weak picture.

'I wanted to stay at home, but it got too hard once my mum had gone. I think it's like self-preservation. That's why I had to leave. I can't get what I need from that sort of love.'

The girl's honesty hits Betty like a dart; far too intimate and delicate for a human with a mindset like hers. The older woman feels sweat sting her palms and her fingers tingle, so balls the caught words up tight, as if written on paper, and throws them back in a bark. She asks no questions, for she barely lets Chloe's words infiltrate her consciousness, but has her reply ready in a whip,

'Yes, that would make sense. Just like I said. Put your own needs first, your generation. You remind me of a student nurse I once had. Gosh! It must have been over thirty years ago! But I can recall her face sharply. And you hold the exact same expression on your face when you harden up and try to shut down. Insolence. Yes, I know your type. She was as green as they come…came from packing carrots for God's sake! She got a terrible report for her first placement, so I told her a few home truths. How she got past her interview I'll never know! How her face fell.'

Chloe regards the twitched, bitter woman long enough to ask what happened to the student but, although it's too hard for Betty to read Chloe's closed expression, she feels undoubtedly judged and possibly hated. She takes delight therefore in boasting of her ability to strip the student nurse bare with her words and leave her wanting to leave, 'She did quit not long after.'

'I wonder if that was her chance. Maybe things could have got better for her, given time? What did her face look like when you told her she was no good?' Chloe looks out of the window while she talks, obviously struggling to continue in the company of her host.

'It crumbled!' But the joy expressed is hollow and Betty fears that Chloe has seen through her factitious display; that some miniscule particle has betrayed her as it floats from her eyes like an escaped dust mote. 'Help me carry the boxes to the attic,' she snaps.

Some photos slide from the top of an overfilled box. Grabbing at them Betty sways a little, taken aback by the image retrieved in her hand.

'You alright? Look like you've seen a ghost.' Again, Chloe's voice is steady and calm.

For once, Betty's immediate response isn't to snap and she allows herself a truer, dreamier tone, 'Just a memory…too long ago.'

'Can I see?' presses Chloe, gingerly, 'she looks pretty. Was she your sister or a friend perhaps?'

'I've no siblings. This was a friend.'

They hear the sitting room clock chime the hour and its timing is uncanny. It's like time's been called on the truth. Betty looks torn, as if she longs to share more, but urgently buttons herself back up. 'You wouldn't understand. Things are different now. We had standards then and standards were everything.'

'How do standards get mixed up with friendship? Did you deny yourself a friend? Was it because of your parents? Would they have disapproved?'

'You ask far too many questions, young lady. I'll do the rest of this myself, thank you,' and she uses her sarcastic thanks to shove this intruder, this damaging soft, caring being, out of her view.

As Betty returns to her kitchen, she feels Arnold watching her, 'Overhear all you like. You can't tell on me anymore! You're just a bird. An old, grey bird that hasn't much life.'

'Just a bird,' chirps the parrot and she imagines he winks at her.

⁂

A FEW WEEKS HAVE PASSED, and a sort of equilibrium has settled over the house. Although sitting far apart, the two women are now unmasked as they watch the evening news together companionably. The end of Lockdown is thought to be in sight and announcements mention the return to normality for the homeless.

'Good news for you, hey! I should be out of your hair maybe by next week, from what they're saying tonight. I reckon you're going to miss me when I go!'

'How we've managed!' Betty shakes her head, ignoring the girl's humour, but demonstrates a less aggressive air. She walks hesitantly to her side cupboard but pulls a photo out of the drawer with purpose, as if her decision to do so can't be denied. Chloe turns to see the friend that Betty mentioned before now being allowed air, as she is propped against the lamp.

'I'm glad you kept that photo aside. She obviously meant a lot to you.'

'I miss her more now than I ever did. Well, in a different way. More like a deep ache than the acute pain of a fresh injury. I spent all those years dressing wounds and yet never attended my own.'

Chloe braves a question that she feels is rhetorical, 'Did you love her?'

Something has shifted in Betty, and it catches her unaware. She feels confused by her vulnerability but for once entertains it, 'Things were so different then. But I know Barbara shouldn't be hidden anymore.'

Retrieving a newspaper cutting from the same drawer, Betty passes it to Chloe and braves the exposure of her long-hidden sexuality, 'She died protesting. She wanted to tell the world who she was, what she believed in. Barbara was much braver than me. She always seemed so much more capable. I suppose her being older by ten years gave her a world view I hadn't yet truly reached.'

The rarity of Betty's gentler reflections delivers her face with a transient warmth and instead of shying from the release of such previously terrifying territory, she sits back in her armchair and gently fondles the comfort of the chenille throw. It occurs to her how sensitive and generous Chloe has been to her these last few weeks. So many times, Betty has snapped and snarled, her eyes sharpened like her opinionated views, 'You have been so accepting of me... my... well, everything.'

'I learnt that from my mum. She would always try to listen; see other people's point of view. Her own childhood was complicated, but she gained a lot of empathy from it. Or maybe that was just part of her; her insides were good.'

'You must miss her.' Betty reinstates her physically distance by sitting up straighter, tightening her stance, while supporting herself with her veined hands tight grasp of the armrests. A well-known dread fills her mind as fear of intimacy sweeps through her like electricity. Confronting the feeling is new ground for her; her tone as unfamiliar to her throat as the concern creeping into her eyes. Saliva fills her mouth.

'Every day. She er...she was too fragile for this world. She couldn't believe in herself. Took her life when I was twelve.' Chloe's speech is steady, and her eyes deflect any pity, but the sadness her words evoke returns the old woman's mind to advisory. As the judgmental cloud greys Betty's face, Chloe is quick to address it, 'Don't judge her. Like I said, her life was complicated.'

Shooting her hand into her front jean's pocket, Chloe pulls out a delicate and minute material bag, suitable for gifting a small piece of jewellery. It has a drawstring and is made of sheer fabric, but the photo on the worn scrap of paper it contains is infinitely more valuable than any precious gem or metal, 'She was called Lisa. Here, this is my mum.'

Betty looks from the photo to the girl several times as her mind's siren wails and she jerks with the unexpected shock treatment; the instant switch floods her brain with cold, steel light. The cause, a single spoken word; the name 'Lisa' released to hover like an imminent crushing atmosphere. In silent horror, Betty realises that this Lisa is that very same student nurse she talked of from years before.

Her strained smile breaks before it reaches Chloe, and Betty needs to support her outstretched arm with the other, like scaffolding, to shakenly return the photo to its owner. Mumbling something incoherent, Betty indicates that she's forgotten something in the kitchen and rushes out to hide her shame. She can't control the tide of long-awaited tears that spill, threatening to drown her. As she feels suffocated by a tsunami of guilt and foolishness, consumed by the acknowledgement of her immense spite, Arnold grabs his opportunity,

'Just old grey bird. Not much life.'

AUTUMN 1963: FACT

hy she had thought a heel of any description would be suitable in Yorkshire now defied all logic. Being brought up in the Fens, her previous review of footwear stopped at muddy or dry. Cobbled declines and steep brick steps were never a consideration. She glared at her almond-toed T-straps and rubbed at her twisted ankle. She hated to be last minute and was furious with herself as she hobbled to the carriage door, pulling it sharply open to hear the whistle blow as soon as the door thud shut behind her. She was immediately engulfed by a flash of panic seeing her lone passenger was male and felt sharply self-conscious as she swopped the offending shoes for her flat and beloved Mary Janes. Ideally, she would have rested her foot on the opposite seat, but the other passenger was male and therefore a potential predator. She positioned herself deliberately opposite him, so to appear less intimidated.

It was hard to say where that assumption of danger was developed. Whether nature or nurture plants such predisposed ideas was a constant debate in heated discussions with her fellow psychology students. The expectation of a

14

woman's gender was never more explicitly demonstrated than by the advertisements and media presentation thrust upon society, now that radio and television were so accessible. Society's insistence that their role is fundamentally in the home or in one of a nibble of jobs, was a weighty argument to explain their subservient nature. But she felt, explicitly, that a woman's identity was caste the moment Eve was presented as an explanation and so gifting Adam the upper hand. The sexual power a man had in owning the object to be placed in the women, rather than the other way round, only emphasized his dominance still further, as did a man's usual leverage in size and strength.

The woman detected a faint but distinct scent which she struggled to name. It must be soap or aftershave but it was a lone strand of ingredient and felt unsatisfying. Yes, the smell seemed incomplete and hard to detect as a whole; like a lone note from a tune, impossible to accurately place.

Settling to read, she felt his eyes on her before she raised her own from her book to check it was so. Her primeval wariness vanished just as swiftly on realising he was studying her book's jacket rather than her face. His eyes caught hers, and after a fractional pause, a flash moment of consideration and evaluation, a wisp of interest was detected in each pair of eyes and an unspoken acceptance exchanged.

'Are you studying for a degree or reading for your personal interest?' the stranger began. His voice was deep and rich which was, in itself, oddly reassuring. Her consideration of him had been gathered swiftly on entering the carriage, knowing that the two of them would be alone in there at least until Malton. She had registered that station while travelling to Scarborough yesterday but couldn't remember how long the stretch was between them. The likelihood of him being a pervert or murderer was further removed when he had raised his hat to acknowledge her arrival. He looked well past middle-age and impeccably dressed. Private, too, as he sank comfortably into his seat and opened his Times; further demonstrating his likely education and probable employment in a respectable career. Safe enough. Also, it was light and would be for a couple more hours. This, perhaps the most inherent of her brain's guidance, had played a large factor in her intuitive conclusion. Her appraisal of the situation had taken less than ten seconds. Possibly three.

She lowered the book to her lap, whilst admitting that she was at Leeds studying psychology. Intuition was one of this semester's topics, but her interest in it reached beyond mere necessity. His smile was open and met with his name on his lips,

'Ted Cuthbert. A like-minded soul no doubt. I am a professor of psychology in Manchester. I am visiting colleagues in Leeds to see how we may incorporate some lectures, for those studying for their masters. I have a fondness for Leeds,' he added with an inviting warmth.

'But you travel from Scarborough not Manchester?' she puzzled aloud, rather than offering her name in exchange.

'Yes,' he amicably replied. 'My work is currently intense and so I have enjoyed a well-earned break by the sea.' His hair was youthful in its volume, and he displayed an academic air as he habitually raked his hand through it and looked almost bashful in his capabilities, 'Do you know this area well?'

'No, not at all. It was my first visit to Scarborough, but I think I'll return.'

'So, you have enjoyed your stay. We were fortunate to see it in such bright weather. I love this time of year for the unexpected nature of its hotter days. So often August lets us down, being surprisingly cold, whereas October can deliver us with gems of heat. You are very fair and so no doubt have to be careful not to burn.'

She smiled, but felt his line a tad too familiar and so bent the conversation to that of a less physical topic, 'I'm reading 'The Tenant of Wildfell Hall' and found myself wanting to visit Anne Bronte's grave.'

'I hadn't realised she is buried in Scarborough. Why not at Haworth I wonder?'

'I've read her relationship was often strained with Charlotte. Maybe Scarborough gave her peace. She was of course very ill by the time she travelled there, in hope of rehabilitation perhaps.'

'You have obviously studied her well. What is it in her writing that you like the most?' Ted's interest was refreshing and the girl felt her shoulder's relax as she fell into the conversation.

'Anne was so unafraid to challenge society and her writing beautifully demonstrates her refusal to constrain her female protagonists. I find her writing so moving and powerful in its recognition of a woman's strengths, and all they have been historically denied, that I felt compelled to honour her memory and visit her grave.' In a few words, she had dispensed far more detail about herself than intended to her lone traveller. Feeling exposed, she again tried to deflect attention from herself, 'Have you read any of her work?'

'I have, as it happens, read The Tenant of Wildfell Hall. I know that book very well as it was, coincidently, one of my daughter's favourites. She said I wouldn't relate to it.' His memory made him chuckle. An obviously fond, deep memory that was allowed to rise and become part of the conversation to this unknown woman, 'You will be of a similar age to hers then, challenging her father! She said I would sympathise with Helen's rogue husband…was it Huntington? I can't remember his Christian name now.'

'Arthur. And did you?'

'Heavens, no! Sylvia, my daughter, had presumed that I would psychoanalyse his reasons for hiding behind his drink, for shamelessly belittling those he claimed to love. That I would somehow excuse his disruptiveness and cruelty. I remember being pained that she would not consider me intuitively aware of my gut response, rather than supposing I would take an educated stance.' She lost him for a moment while he reflected on this past situation, and she supposed something had been left undone. As she watched him regain his previous ease, his eyes reflected the light and seemed to sparkle a little mischievously. He continued the conversation playfully, 'Which rather leads to your present studies again, doesn't it? Just how much should we allow our intuition to guide the many judgements we have to make each day?'

The train jolted as it screeched a little at its station stop. No one entered their carriage, and she was pleased, as the conversation was interesting to her, and she had hoped it wouldn't be interrupted.

'For instance,' he continued, 'I note that you feel it best not to share your name with me.' He smiled with warm, genuine encouragement, seeming to demonstrate he neither sought it nor judged her decision and was only merely making an observation, 'I think that this is your intuitive response to being alone in a carriage with an unknown male stranger. A name has a power to it. An incredible one, when we examine that closely. But here, in this instance, it may be to protect your privacy, for I had already divulged to you that I am in the Manchester faculty for the very subject you study. That link may feel a little too close. Intimate. Intimacy can appear incredibly dangerous to instinct. That alone could have made you flee, move to a different carriage as soon as a chance became available.' He laughed fondly, leaning back deeper into his seat's mock tweed fabric, rubbing the back of his head on the headrest.

'It's true! Although decided at a sub-conscious level which, of course, only proves your diagnosis absolutely! My fear of flight has now been sufficiently removed to allow me to release 'Barbara',' and, with this omission, she extended her un-gloved hand with purpose, to demonstrate her own mental adequacies. 'I have often wondered just how many times a day we act instinctively but, to be honest, it requires such a meticulous level of study that I'm lost to it within a few hours. It must be many more times than we're aware of, as often so subtle. Even intangible.'

'Without a doubt. And yet, the degree of intuitive behaviour varies vastly between individuals. There's been an interesting study by Americans, Myers and Briggs. Have you come across it yet? They are unusually a mother and daughter team, notably with no psychological training, I should add. But fascinating in the accuracy of their results. Myers is due to present their findings at the American Psychological Association conference next year and I hope to be there. They have formatted a questionnaire which can detect 16 personality types, based on the theory of psychological types produced by Carl Gustav Jung.'

'No doubt it will be covered once more widely released. I am reading around the subject of 'intuition' in preparation. I should mention that I'm only just starting my second year,' Barbara said apologetically, as if disclosing disadvantages and failings.

'Your knowledge is far from inept, my dear. You demonstrate great promise.'

They fell into a companiable silence, each engrossed in their reading material with the only interruption a barely registered turn of the page, or occasional repositioning of legs. At one point, Barbara looked up to puzzle a point just read and her attention was drawn to his newspaper. It looked oddly old but was positioned so that the headlines and date were not possible to see. She noted the peculiarity and turned to look outside. The sun had lost its battle with the clouds. Now the wind moved with determination, shoving the previous cottonwool fluff out of the way to be replaced by a blanket of grey, driving any suggestion of the previous blue to memory.

After some time, she noticed Ted was gazing out of the window looking rather lost in his thoughts. His eyes suggested he looked beyond the beautiful Yorkshire landscape and so it was hard to distinguish if it was the terrain his expression pined for, or something long lost. As he turned his gaze to hers, a tiredness was demonstrated on his previously youthful demeanour.

'In a way I envy you,' he shared honestly. 'There is no excitement like the first coming to things. No taste so sharp, pain so felt, word so piercing, as the one that shall mould your future path.'

'Are those your own words? I like them.' She unwrapped biscuits from their aluminium foil. Hoping that they weren't serendipitously broken and going to embarrass her when being picked out, she offered one to her travelling companion with a slight nod of invitation.

'Thank you, I will.' Accepting a custard cream, he returned his gaze to her, 'Yes, my words. They come from years of reflection. Years of observation. Years of listening to harrowing stories and regrets that only a human can store and hold onto for such little purpose.' He laughed briefly, but not happily, more to dispel the heaviness of his words and effortlessly steered the conversation to a different course, 'Imagine if I had sneezed or coughed once our train had moved off. What would your instinct have told you to do?'

'Well, I expect it would rather depend on how you did it. If you'd sprayed me with germs, I would have been repulsed and looked after myself, rather than politely enquiring after your health. I'm very glad that you didn't,' she added with humour and honesty.

'You would have been annoyed rather than terrified?'

'But of course. I can see no place for terror in that scenario.'

'What if I'd said I am suffering from the flu? Would a level of fear have arisen in your instant reaction?'

'No. I'm sure it wouldn't have been fear, but irritation for sure. I wouldn't want the inconvenience of catching it.'

'So, you would presume that it was only an inconvenience and keep it within context. But what if this exchange had happened and you had noticed the headline on my Times was 'Killer Flu reaches Epidemic Proportions?'

Barbara considered this for a moment. She knew that he was seeking her reaction to his use of 'killer' and 'epidemic' and was slightly reluctant to admit that the headline would adversely affect her intuition. She naturally fell into student role, as she explored his proposal, 'Killer impregnates fear as does Epidemic; something so contagious that we should put measures in place to avoid it. How many people have actually died from it? It may bring no more threat to healthy people than any other flu but an epidemic suggests it may somehow become unmanageable.'

'Exactly what I would have observed. Now, imagine the word 'pandemic' in the headline. Start to hear it on every news bulletin, a daily death toll, each country's statistics, and you do feel the force of a monster of terror? Of losing control? But, still, it's the same flu which you previously only felt irritated by. The use of language and media coverage on any given circumstance or topic, can alter one's intuitive response. I'm sure it's totally over-ridden in those who don't observe it in their daily lives; and yet it can make those that are more intuitively inclined, doubt themselves and become muddled and unclear in their definitive.'

'And so leading to a state of ambiguity?'

'Precisely. A whole nation could be controlled fairly swiftly, I expect, by stripping them of their basic and essential natural instinct.' His eyes seemed larger as he emphasized his words.

For some reason the word 'stripping' made her momentarily uncomfortable and aware of her vulnerabilities. Recovering herself, she returned to the thread last spoken, 'These are dark and troublesome thoughts. It's pretty horrifying to consider. It sounds very much like a form of brain control. Like in Orwell's Nineteen Eighty-Four.'

They let consideration sit amongst their silence and Barbara sensed he was savouring her obvious digestion of something new to her. He drew closer, bridging the gap between opposite seats, 'Imagine the effects if it was a worldwide control. Would it be the end of civilisation as we know it?' He confided his deepest thoughts in a whisper, and she felt she detected a sinister tone but then rationalised it was just the bleakness of her own thoughts.

It was with relief that she raised her head to see the approach of Pendas Way. The twin-platformed station was hard to distinguish in the now late afternoon drizzle of their once fine October day.

'Gosh!' she said, sharply pulling her gloves on and hurriedly placing her book in her handbag. 'I hadn't realised we were talking for so long. This is my stop.' Reaching for her overnight bag, Ted swiftly retrieved it for her. She registered that it was oddly the only bag on the overhead rack.

'Thank you. It was a pleasure to meet you, Ted.'

'I get off here too,' he gestured that she exit the door that he now held open for her.

'I thought you were travelling to Leeds Centre. This does go all the way through.' For a second, instinct rippled up her spine, but she lay an imaginary hand on it, chiding its appearance at such an unnecessary time. Stepping onto the platform, she felt him immediately behind her.

'I need to get off here,' he said decisively, sharing no further detail.

'But you have no bag' she thought, whilst trying to unscramble the significance of this.

The station was left in silence once the train had moved away. A crow briefly flew low but passed through, seeing no morsels to pick and no reason to stay. The drizzle persisted, leaving a faintly atmospheric mist.

'Pendas Way,' Ted stated, indicating the signpost marking the station. 'It's being demolished next year. Did you know?'

'You're remarkably well informed on things that aren't in your area,' she tried to make the comment light, jovial, but the change in her mood blocked it. Why did he suddenly seem menacing?

'I keep my eyes and ears open, don't like to miss a trick. I have been likened to a fox before now,' he laughed.

'I'm not sure that that's a compliment.' Her mouth felt dry.

'I'm sure it wasn't meant as one.' Was it her imagination or had he deliberately snarled those words?

She felt oddly frozen. She knew she should be walking away but considered the path from the station, which was isolated and hidden until it joined the road.

'Do you live on Pendas Way?' His tone demanding in its enquiry.

'Just up from it. Not at all far from here. My flatmates will be wondering where I am. I must leave.' Her voice had lost its authority, but she was aware she must appear unfrazzled. The ease of her previous conversation with this same man had left with the train and was now replaced by something else. Something that made little sense to her and which she was unwilling to entertain. She squashed it down every time it tried to flash, pushing its warning into her consciousness, but she did allow a silent acknowledgment that she was grateful to be in her flat Mary Janes, and that her ankle's throb had calmed down.

He stepped in front of her, as if insisting they must talk more, 'It's so quiet round here.' His gaze moved to the farmland opposite, accessed by crossing the lattice foot-bridge at the north end. He turned his head to take in the few house backs, a distance from them on the main road. 'What does your intuition tell you now?' His voice was as deep and eloquent as before, but the previous warmth was replaced with the arrogance of academia, the advantage of a superior, and hinted at punishment for such insolent stupidity.

'I have to go,' was blurted with little control as she found herself pacing wide and hard, frantic to leave the platform for the narrow path, rather than displaying the confidence she wanted to suggest. She knew there were gardens on both sides of the worn, high wooden fences edging the path, so she may not be as alone as she feared. She could scream.

But when he grabbed her, his hand clamped her mouth with such strength that she felt her knees buckle and her plan to kick out and yell was as much lost as her mental purpose.

'Everything I've told you about myself may have been a lie,' his face was contorted as he lowered her to the ground, still far from the road and her imagined freedom. His voice harsh and wicked, 'I'm not going to hurt you. You can relax. I just want you to understand. Appreciate the gift that you have and yet choose to deny. There is nothing… nothing, as essential as our instinct. Imagine an animal without it. Imagine having no idea when to run, to hunt, your awareness. Let go of your preconceived ideas of acceptable and 'safe'. Listen to your gut.'

Leaving her shaking amongst some shards of glass, cigarette butts and dandelions, he sleekly disappeared into the encroaching haze. By the time she had staggered to the road, there was no trace of him. Feeling immense panic that he may reappear and follow her home, she clumsily staggered and stumbled, not able to grace her legs with the swift steps she willed them to create. Tripping on kerbs and twitching at each sound, hugging walls, and stepping closer to other walkers, she reached the safety of her empty flat.

TED CUTHBERT

*I*t was frustrating to Charles Simpson to have to release a false name. He was immensely proud of the attachments his given name had accumulated over the years; a hard-earned reputation, not easily or quickly presented, and it irked him to hide it. It was his habit over the last few years, to throw a false name out willy-nilly and hope that he could remember his invention. To respond at least to the Christian name, if not the last. He therefore always chose a one syllable Christian name as his lie, and so it was Ted Cuthbert who now introduced himself to the young woman opposite.

He observed that her own name was not returned, and noted this as a rather exciting development, suggesting an intelligence and possible strength of character not often observed in one of his objects. The position she had taken on the opposing seat made them unusually face-to-face, indicating to him she was possibly unthreatened or had a challenging nature.

He had considered her aura when she burst into the carriage, her age, expression, and reaction to his presence.

He had noted her lack of make-up in contrast to her fashionable clothes, as she lifted her overnight bag to the upper rack, and her figure, out of habit, for he recognised the animal trait in him to observe such things despite making no further mental image of what would lie beneath them. That wasn't his thing, although he anticipated the pleasure produced from fine lines and soft firm skin. It was mind games that fed his need. To overpower and ultimately defeat another's mind, that vulnerable human necessity.

The fact that his fellow passenger studied psychology made the natural course of conversation a little too easy for him to fully engage in and so he detoured from it as soon as possible, helped by her willingness to share her love of Anne Bronte. And what were the chances of that! Not only to mention the author but to refer to the same novel at the heart of one of his most prized and deliciously fresh memories.

Sylvia, his daughter, had been so unusually verbally aggressive when she had bravely challenged his character and dared to compare him to the callous Huntington, Bronte's devil. She had, of course, allowed emotion to seep into her passion, and so weakened her stance entirely and at an annoyingly early interval. But what fun it had been to turn her views back on her with suggestions of guilt and shame, the most powerful of his tools, and watch them pick at and ultimately destroy what she thought she knew. The years it had taken to patiently mould and confuse her judgements; such a tricky balance to give precisely enough affection so as not to rob the possibility that he, her father, must genuinely care for her. Despite such blatant disregard. Despite such measured hostility.

He looked back to the woman opposite, well barely much more than a girl, fresh-faced and beautifully caught in a ray of sunlight. He wanted her name and got it through artful subtle mocking, playful fondling suggestion, whilst reinforcing his own confidence. Barbara. The touch of her small hand in his alerted him to her vulnerability, like a switch on a horse's back. How wonderfully caressing. He gave her some superior knowledge to check the scales were as they should be and sank into stroking his ego with contemplations that rejuvenated him like the fragrance of fresh-cut spring grass.

He had known no students by Barbara's name, but she reminded him a little of a girl called Annie; one of his first affairs, back in the late twenties when he was perhaps thirty, and Annie ten years his junior. One that he had abandoned once her belly had swelled too much in her pregnancy's third trimester. He had heard that her family had had her admitted to the local asylum, as choosing to be a single mother was deemed a grave illness, even then. Even until the fifties. A sickness of the mind and a problem to be squashed. Repelled. It was rather amusing to him how long society had maintained this seemingly Victorian view, but he welcomed the new age of contraception as much as any of the emerging hippies he now met.

Why his women always believed he actually wanted a child, there and then, was beyond his comprehension. Could they not see his lifestyle was free and his appetite fed by an artful game of spinning plates of uncompromised and deliciously uncommitted edibles? He made his wife, his daughters known to them; it increased the tempo, the desire. Did they really think he would forfeit such a carefully organised web simply to be ensnared by another woman? If he demonstrated a regard for children or disclosed a desire to one day have more, it was only to draw them further in. To catch their hearts more completely. For that suggestion always seized their minds, weakened their perspective. But why did they always claw so willingly at his hint of a future? He was entirely blameless. If his natural good looks and charm trapped them into choosing to believe he loved them, and that they could mean more to him than mere entertainment, how could he convince them otherwise? This was one area in which the female mind had defeated him. For no matter how obvious his cruelty, how discourteous his manner, how blatant his cheating, these women still appeared to hold love in their hearts for him. Remained annoyingly clingy.

Aware his thoughts were digressing, he returned to the slim female opposite, so obviously not actually reading the content of the pages she scanned but wanting to appear so. He imagined her thoughts really sank into a delicious bath of bubbles containing her intriguing travelling companion. He imagined her touching herself, with thoughts of his weight on her, the scent of his salty skin. He pictured the surge of her warm, fragranced bath water lap on her thighs as her desire climaxed with her breath full of heat. He relished that she most likely wanted to be touched by him; imagined her delight if he were to stretch out to rid the distance between them. That she would come to sit on his lap and try to be babied. Held.

If he could have picked a name for Barbara it would have been Audrey, as in Audrey Hepburn. For her piled hair and pencilled brows had immediately brought the actress to his mind. And those ridiculous little heels that she had limped in on, interestingly replaced and now stored away. Now Audrey Hepburn would be fun to play with if she really were as sparky as depicted in her films. He might take it too far with her though, he shuddered with delight as his gifted imagination supplied him with a brief and delicious image of Audrey Hepburn nakedly writhing on his bed.

Tired of this thought, he considered where his authority had first taken shape, once returned from France a little worse for trench conditions and tied to a young bride through the determination of her parents. A pregnancy to be stillborn as it happened. He had automatically acquired an air of superiority when taking his post at Manchester University in the late twenties. It had just been given, handed to him with the territory and, although proving incredibly useful later, he had at first rather despised the willingness of his students to presume him more knowledgable and experienced than themselves. Serving in the First World War had left him wiser, more rounded, but for God's sakes! He wasn't that much their senior. Why did so many search for a supportive rod, seem to need a guardian and mentor to escort them on their paths. Why were they so unable to fly free and have no ties, no burdens?

His peers were much more guarded and required courting and demonstrative proof, suspicious of such ease in one's skin and his relaxed approach to the starched nature of academia. They poked for discrepancies and listened for rumour but eventually fell too for his warmth and enveloping character. They too became idle in their contentment to regard him an expert, a rare find. Even the oldest ones, presuming their years would beat his wit and sharp observations, succumbed to bend the knee, bowing to his astuteness and craft.

But it was whilst an inmate, from the age of forty-eight, that his passion for mind games and dominance had really exploded his senses. All the damaged souls he met whilst inside, that sought him out to confide in; so open in their vulnerabilities, so stark in their own hunger, and nearly always unguardedly allowing their own minds to devour their sensibilities. It was a true feast for someone as predisposed as he, and his reputation spread quickly, in whispers

31

through brick wall and canteen queues. There was someone they could talk to. Someone who would listen. Much more rewarding than the tiresome creatures who lay on his psychotherapy coach these days; woman struggling with affairs, menopause, children flying the nest. He detested being a psychotherapist in middle-class suburbia, but he had no choice but to be self-employed since his well-broadcast fall from grace.

The prisoners' willingness to share intimate details of their damaging childhoods or horrific crimes, to beg for charity, redemption, a chance to change, never failed to astound him. Or the ones so filled with hate and anger that a chisel was needed to forge some sort of path where Charles could later implant his own influence. He met few who showed no remorse or conscience but, when he did, his mouth wet with saliva, his heart quickened and skin prickled. It was a feeling to savour and an awareness to bathe in, anticipating the long haul of courtship required to conquer such a similarly charged mind.

He wished he could share his story a little with this Barbara, suddenly saddened that he must deny himself this joy. How she would stare with her over large eyes as he told of his wrong doings, classed as manipulation by the courts, exploitation, and corruption, with his entangled embezzlement of state money actually nailing him the sorry sentence of ten years.

For a time, he allowed his thoughts to become stuck on the aftermath of this period, so much so that an onlooker could have been mistaken him as reflective. But he was simply lost in a moment of self-pity, remembering his wife and girls striding from him, as if leaving a nasty stain on a once-loved rug. Rolling it up in eventual acceptance that it wouldn't wash out, could not be removed, and thinking it therefore best discarded.

He remembered each of his conquests' names, only ever female, that he had chosen and groomed and overpowered so easily. It was perhaps a mistake when his hunger had detoured from the all-giving, blinded-by-love wimp women he selected. Most of his peers had proved just as gullible as the flouncy students, but a certain Elizabeth Marrs, crisply ironed and sweet as the syrup poured over steaming pancakes, had proved his match. That still wounded him to say. Knowing that he couldn't engulf her, detect her vulnerabilities, and dominate, frustrated him still. After so many years, he still hungered for the satisfaction of knowing that she could be made to need him more than she needed herself. But, he supposed, she'd perhaps have a disadvantaged, aged mind by now, and so wouldn't be worth finding.

He looked again to his now dated Times and digested the words he loved to re-read endlessly. The article had been written by a pompous literate but resulted in a yarn of disparaging words that delighted Charles's senses. Deviant, bamboozle, expropriate, mesmerising. Aahhh. He stretched his shoulders back to fill his chest with the descriptives and gazed through the window. His eyes caught Barbara's in the reflection, and he threw her a thought.

What a homely being she is, with her attempts to be mature with neatly packaged, boring biscuits. The worst thing she most likely anticipates is that they have broken on the journey. How he would love to shake her world up, fire some guns, rock her boat. Watch her response. Hoping that for once the result would be unanticipated and require

33

complex reasoning to appreciate. But she, like so many before her, used her known intelligence and well-understood responses as her route for her meagre lane of life. She appeared to play safe, taking no outside road to cut him off. She could have denied him the opportunity of taking charge, driving the conversation. She's mentioning Orwell, his head groaned. Yawn, yawn. So, she's read Nineteen Eighty-Four. He ramped it up by moving to her, thus allowing her to feel his physical presence and stoked some ash in his heart's pit in doing so; to ignite a sad, sparse flame. He detected an instant quickening of her breath, her eyes dash. His tone and encroachment have unsettled her. Excellent.

Only travelling to the sea for a day out he had no need for more than his well-loved briefcase, full of articles he'd published when employed at Manchester and memorabilia from his court case, his favourite newspaper coverage and meaningful tickets or appointment slips. He snapped the metal clasps down to enclose what he regarded as his ultimate newspaper triumph, front page coverage on the 1948 Times. And it took him by surprise, on vacating the train, that Barbara had only just registered his lack of luggage in the overhead rack.

He'd play with her just a little, just to scramble her thoughts sufficiently to disturb her and plant a darkness that it seemed she would benefit from nurturing. He couldn't be long. Getting off here meant he would need to get a taxi to the centre now and he didn't want to put Deidre off with late behaviour. It was too early in their relationship to appear obviously careless, and Deidre's wealth was of much greater significance to him than this two-bit girl standing petrified on the platform.

The ease of his dominance was outstanding, even to him on reflection. His effortless prowl, the almost quiescent nature of Barbara's response, the dexterity of his accomplishment, ensured he wouldn't need to create any commotion with Deidre later to sleep well tonight.

FEN TO HILL AND BACK AGAIN

*E*lizabeth Marrs was cleaning out her closet. This physical exercise would, unwittingly, lead to a mental spring-clean, too. As bags were labelled 'bin', 'charity' or 'Susi', no allowance was made for memorabilia. Elizabeth was almost seventy, so allowances had been discarded long ago.

Her cousin Susi, ten years younger and with two working daughters, never missed the chance to accept Elizabeth's cast-offs. A true 'Marrs' trait, to never overlook a possibility. Over the years, there had been some quality clothing passed down, both fashionable and suitable for her daughters' office roles. The years that Elizabeth had spent working at Manchester University hadn't been long but had seen her wardrobe enriched with well-chosen finds and homemade garments from the best Yorkshire wools. She had dressed sharply, in classics that were still appreciated, albeit with a little alteration.

Elizabeth laughed out loud thinking what Susi's daughters would say when they saw the shoulder pads in the jacket she held before her. The monster shapes shamed any contemporary attempt at the statement. 'What do these eighties kids know!' she chuckled to herself. But, pulling out the next piece, a pretty, ruffled blouse stuffed deliberately to the very back of the cupboard, her smile was instantly erased. Elizabeth held it first at a distance, as if it was harmful and shouldn't be touched, before bringing it close to her, hugging it, and breathing its memory as she closed her eyes and submitted to something clearly painful.

'I thought I'd burnt you,' she muttered, shaking its creases, and holding it up before her. The feminine, chiffon top had aged well, helped by its synthetic protection from moths, 'You've not even faded, kept so dark. The blues are just as I remember them.'

She took a moment, not because she doubted that this blouse would be placed in the bin bag but because she was floored by the memory box it had forced her to open. Stuffing the overspilled contents of that unwelcome break back into a far corner of her mind, she continued briskly with her work.

'Elizabeth. Liz. I've pee'd the bed again,' came her mother's call from her bed in the sitting room.

'I'll be one minute, Mum. Don't worry, the clean sheets should be dry by now.'

⁂

THE AIR WAS BEGINNING to dampen as the late February sun readied to set. It had been a fine day and weather which Elizabeth had been very grateful for. The pile of sheets and towels had steadily accumulated, waiting for a sun generous enough with its heat. Her mother's UTI had caused most of the accidents, but she had been on antibiotics for over four days so they should surely have knocked it on the head by now? She thought about calling her

37

cousin Betty in Felixstowe, for some nursing advice, but quickly decided against it. She didn't want to hear the judgement in her nasal voice or be antagonised by any reference to her mother having 'made her bed'. Well, she had never imagined making her bed full of wee, had she? Elizabeth ironically thought. Why her cousin, younger by thirty-five years, had to be so cold and detached had always puzzled Elizabeth, but she knew that a relationship with the woman was never going to be possible.

She supposed, as she pulled the pegs from the line, that this was all part of the tumour's spread. Her mother had got the scan results last month which showed secondaries now ate her brain. Elizabeth had imagined them like the Pacman one of her niece's boys had shown her on their TV. Thousands upon thousands of cells reluctantly waiting in line to be gobbled and eradicated by an ever-increasing monster. Sense was bound to be attacked, along with memory and functionality and all the other faculties which were the very mum of her Mum.

Elizabeth looked past the wooden fence surrounding their garden. The dark row of conifers closed any view from the back. She hated them. Always had. Oppressive and totally unnecessary in her opinion. But mother had always kept them, as if honouring the wants of Elizabeth's absentee father. Like insisting that Elizabeth keep his surname; owning none of its shameful attachments but instead cherishing what she saw as the splendour of having once been his.

'He planted them to break the wind. He would have loved to have seen them standing so tall,' was the constant reply if an opinion was ever aired.

'Loved to see nothing then?' Elizabeth would glare. Why her mother had any respect for the scoundrel she had to name 'Dad' was beyond her. She had few memories of him, and those that she held, all consisted of a dominating, red-faced bull of a man. It seemed he'd had the regard of a terrorist and the gentleness of the Fen Tiger that he was. By the time she had turned five, he was locked up. He had driven a spade into the foot of a mate, saying it would be his head next time. Elizabeth had heard that he had been protecting her mum's honour; something had been said. 'He was always there for me, your dad,' would be a regular line from her mum, as Elizabeth grew into her teenage years. But, when he failed to come home once released, it seemed unlikely that this was quite the case to an increasingly sharp-witted daughter. As far as they knew, he had settled in America and went on to run his own 'enterprise' with his brothers on a Caribbean Island. She had heard guns were involved.

With the billowing, fresh sheets folded and piled into the broken plastic basket, a wide expanse of arable field was exposed before her across the road to the front of their house. Field after field after field; only divided by a thin line of what she knew to be dyke and differentiated by the colour of their content. Mostly still bare earth at this time of year, but a few showed green promise; crops to justify this land. It was so flat and unmarked that she could see the church tower of the neighbouring village. The uncurving line of Council houses surrounding theirs, which was almost central in its pair, were stark against the wide, watching sky. No matter it's colour or content, the sky was upon them; integrated and woven through the days like a second skin. It reliably affected the growth and work and atmosphere of the land below it. Occasionally, a beautiful evening light would be cast on the house fronts and fields, and Elizabeth would want to capture it. Store it, and let it seep out of her imagined jar on all of the colourless days. The warm gold glow cloaking each of the ordinary and transforming them into something magical.

The semi-detached homes varied not one bit in their build, but most front gardens contained a multitude of discarded items, individual to each home and yet oddly similar. Some had old mattresses or discarded white appliances amongst the weedy gravel or paving along the space at the side. The Coopers even had a pile of junk protruding past their sitting room window, whilst the Halls had a sideboard turned over with the bottom taken out. This was serving as a kennel for their chained dog. A couple of neighbours had speedway cars, bashed and characterful with their slogans painted in glaring colours on every surface. Those were the Jessops. All related one way or another. In fact, she knew her father's family connected her to Ruby next-door; that most of the fen was as good as related, one way or another.

Elizabeth's house stood apart from the others, with its flower boxes on the downstairs windowsills and bordered lawn at the front. There, reliable flowers such as blue lithodora, red salvia and white geraniums displayed a well-rehearsed performance year in, year out. This reflected Elizabeth's mother's fierce belief in 'Loyalty to the Royalty', as she so often laughed. She had been bred that way and had named her daughter to reflect those same resolute principles. Elizabeth's mother was an Ann, her mum's brother an Edward, and his daughter, Elizabeth's cousin, Betty, had been christened as yet one more, 'deep curtesy to the Queen', Elizabeth.

Before the cancer hit her too hard, Elizabeth's mother would kneel down each autumn to tenderly take the geraniums out and place them in the shed, in the hope that some, at least, would survive well enough for a show next year. She was a woman who had pride and rugged determination. It was hard to see her struggling as she now was. The phone call which had brought Elizabeth back two years ago, pulling her in as if she were on a fishing line, helpless to swim away and feeling the pain of a hook in her mouth at the outcome she knew would ensue, had been inevitable. Elizabeth was the only child, and her mum could no longer manage. And she loved her mum.

It was just where her parent had chosen to stay and live her life that Elizabeth struggled to appreciate. Why she hadn't started afresh, moved away. She knew her mum would have loved Yorkshire, she had so often talked about wanting to see hills, climb rocky terrain. But that was years ago, and Elizabeth had given up and settled nearer The Fen once she'd left Manchester, choosing Cambridge as some sort of happy medium. It felt more on the fringe of the flat, haunting land and therefore easier to mingle with society. Not the Fen people. Not them.

Was it because they were her dad's people that she thought so meanly of them? Was it the wound of childhood memories; being teased at school for reading a book, wearing a slightly different style of shoe, pronouncing words properly? Is that why she'd always felt she stood apart? Was an outsider? Because her mum worked in the library rather than a shop or on the fields? These were questions she rarely entertained but today, as she wearily placed the laundry on the kitchen table, she allowed them space. Her mum had always been happy-go-lucky, glad to have a nicer house than the one she had grown up in, and glad to have a job she enjoyed. Independently, she had learnt to drive, saved for a banger, and encouraged her daughter to strive for the best education she could. She had implanted the belief that knowledge was valuable and night after night, had read lent books to her growing girl, full of inspiring and adventurous heroines. Never looking too deep, refusing to explore the 'why's' and 'what-ifs' but creating a superficially smiling world, where pain was blocked. Elizabeth knew her own emotional development had been affected but, appreciating she had much to thank her mother for, she went to join her in the sitting room.

'After we've sorted this, shall we watch some TV?' her mum whispered cheekily. There was a sparkle in her eyes that Elizabeth missed and hadn't seen for some time.

'What are you up to? You never could hide mischief!'

'Nothing. Really, honest,' she raised her hands on weak, slow arms, wiggling the fingers with childlike delight. Her skin looked bruised and saggy. These aren't my mum's arms, thought Elizabeth sadly.

'But it's Saturday night, isn't it? Edmonds will be on,' her mum coyly explained.

Elizabeth couldn't appreciate how Noel Edmonds could liven her mother up so much. She had even stopped hoovering on Saturday mornings to google at him when he'd presented Multi-Coloured Swap Shop. 'It's his hair, I think. Oh, and his blue eyes. Bit like your father, he is,' would be her explanation. 'Was. Maybe,' Elizabeth had thought crossly.

'It's Sunday today, Mum. We watched him last night, didn't we? You knew the answer to that…'

'Oh, no bother. We'll watch it tomorrow then.' And her mum rolled over to help Elizabeth pull the dirtied sheet out from under her.

※

THE NATURE PROGRAMME was the best of a bad bunch. Elizabeth smiled as she watched her mum wriggle like the eels she was watching, totally captivated, and absorbed into the scene.

'I've been dreaming about eels you know. They come through the walls, take over this house! Or is it snakes?' she puzzled out loud. 'Your dad hated snakes, Liz.' Why her mother increasingly pulled him out of her memories these last few months seemed bizarre and slightly cruel for her mother to have to entertain.

'My dad was a snake. You've just chose to forget.'

'Ooh! Crabs!' her mother screamed, as she hid under the sheet from the hundreds of orange, shelly pincers reaching for her from the screen. 'Your dad got crabs. Said it was from borrowing a mate's football shorts. I knew that didn't sound right, but what can you do?'

'What can you do? Oh, Mum. How did you stay with him?'

'Cause I loved him, of course! The Devil that he was.' she chuckled but clouded over as her memory expanded its picture, 'He took me down the doctor. Paid a bob for it. He said he'd seen him already, but I felt I smelt a rat. There I sat, with you on my lap, waiting and waiting; surrounded by locals who I imagined could read why I was there. God, I felt out of place. I remember not feeling 'there' at all, like I'd mentally removed myself.'

'How old would you have been? And me?' Elizabeth felt appalled on so many scales that she was finding it hard to balance them, but she reached for her mum's hand to reassure her; she was in no way going to judge such a difficult time. She stroked the back of her mum's hand with her thumb, and it grounded her, just as it always had as a child.

43

'You were only tiny. Maybe one.'

'So, you weren't much more than a teenager yourself then?'

'No. But I felt grown up. And your dad made me feel special, with him being so well regarded, so I felt odd to be there. I'd never cheated on him of course. Had a clean history but found myself there, waiting like a dirty thing.' She winced at her words and the shame that they brought, and Elizabeth was in two minds to change the subject but her mum continued, in a now rare moment of articulate and astute memory, 'The nurse said they'd look after you while I was examined and took you to another place. Away from me. That still worries me now. I was put in stirrups with my fanny exposed to the door. God, the humiliation. I seemed to wait there, legs up and straddled, for ages. I remember thinking I should free them, sit up and wait for the doctor with some dignity. I'd done nothing wrong.'

'Absolutely, Mum. This is so troublesome. So wrong,' Elizabeth laid her head on her mum's shoulder and tried to steady her own intrusive memories, to concentrate only on her mum's experience. But the similarities were stark, and her empathy hurt. The sharp knock on a closed door of her mind, made her heart beat faster as it awakened a buried thought: I stole my mum's one chance of a grandchild.

'When the doctor came in, he shoved the speculum in without so much as an introduction. He didn't ask one question or utter a single word. I bravely managed to ask why an internal when crabs were all I'd come in for. But he didn't reply, just left the room. Your father was so cross when I did eventually get out of there. It was teatime, 'You've been ages. What have you been doing?' was all he blurted. Hmmm. Funny old memory that one.'

'It's not funny, Mum. It's really sad. But you need to put it to bed now. It's good you spoke it, let it out. Look, I'll go make a cuppa and then we can chat some more.' Elizabeth bent to kiss her mum's forehead as she rose for the kitchen. She was so horrified by the images created by her mum's story that they almost over-rode her own recall of similar events but, by the time the kettle was filled with water and placed to boil, tea bags were in the pot and two mugs retrieved, she stood at the window to let her own memory flood her.

In her mind, she wore the chiffon blouse again and some tailored trousers that she had adored. She had thought it best to dress confidently for such a difficult occasion. She was only twenty-three, determined and assured, but still not long a child. Charles, twenty years her senior, had said he'd come with her, but a vital meeting had come up at the University, which he couldn't possibly miss. She hadn't minded that too much, she felt stronger on her own; less likely to crumple.

The doctor had been similar to the one her mother had just described, the only noises in the sterile room the ping of latex gloves and metal spectrum hitting the tin bowl. There might have been a hum; that low-grade, constant monotone that is barely distinguishable but feels as if the actual atmosphere is quietly crackling in your ears. And there was the clinical smell, the nauseous septic hint. Her decision to have the abortion had taken far longer than the procedure itself. It was so factual that the formality in itself felt like robbery. There was no sense of occasion.

She had never regretted it until these last few years. Seeing her mum slip away from her, feeling the cut of silence more than she ever remembered before, she had allowed her mind to wander; to imagine a make belief child

45

running through the front door to her, cuddling up on the sofa late at night. But the image was always too young; she knew her child would almost be fifty in reality. Most likely with kids of its own…grandchildren for her. Family to continue things once she was gone. To make her own life, and that of her mothers, substantial. She had never allowed herself to consider this before; had felt no hole or space from her singledom.

But there was never any doubt at all in her mind that Charles would not have kept his word. There was no way he would leave his wife, his faithful backdrop and image maker, or ruffle his position at Manchester, despite all his protests that he would set up home with Elizabeth. They'd be a family. Well, one of his. 'Isn't that what she wanted, for God's sakes?' She knew she had confused him; side-stepped his game. What she wanted was not to be controlled by a man. Not to have a disingenuous 'mate' who would never put her first. She didn't want to be with someone like her dad.

Another image came to mind, unwanted but pushing its way to the front of waiting scenes. It was the first time Charles had taken her out. She'd been wearing that same blouse. She remembered it well because she had loved it so much. Charles had been a gentleman, appearing almost bashful and unsure at times. But with a quiet confidence that balanced this and created a most delightful character. His humour had him poke his head a little too far through her front door that first night, as he teased about her wrapping paper wall.

'They aren't bloomin' wrapping paper!' she had laughed, knowing he really appreciated the torn-out Vogue covers and that her sticking them up to brighten the drab hallway was effective and different.

'You like your fashion, don't you?' He had run his eyes over her, slowly, surely, with the confidence of a cat. The game had started. But he had underestimated her strength of character and individuality; thinking her departmental secretarial role reflected some kind of subservience, lesser intelligence, in their shared world of academia.

She stood up straight, from her stance of leaning into the sink; like she had thought she might vomit. She pulled her shoulders back and lifted her chin, 'Bloody man.'

She smarted as she rolled her eyes to the dark line of conifers, that seemed to have moved two feet closer since she entered the kitchen. But a light in their neighbour's shed caught her eye and welcomely distracted her thoughts. It was Bob putting his rabbits to bed. The lad had many hutches, piled four high: probably a good twenty last time she'd gone round there. He was as soft with them as a bloke could be, they were his proper babies. He just loved animals, nothing more. They weren't a unique collection or bred for the plate. He kept them just for love.

He raised his hand to her, caught in the light of her kitchen window, as he made his way down his garden path.

'Forgot the carrots, dinnit I!' he called in self-effacing laughter.

She opened the door a smidge to throw the teabags into her collection for composting,

'You spoil those nibblers!' she told him kindly, aware of his pride in their care.

'You'll have to come over and meet the latest kittens. Just born yesterday they were.'

'How many does that make it?' Although Elizabeth pulled a face of mock concern, she knew as well as he that she

47

had a soft spot for the creatures.

'Twenty-seven now. I lost Charlie last week.'

'Sorry to hear that, Bob. I'll give you a knock in the next few days, Love. You can show me them then. Night, night.'

Tea poured, with some chocolate on the side, Elizabeth entered the sitting room feeling strangely cleansed. As if her mum's account had somehow further strengthened Elizabeth's resolve that she had done what she had needed to do.

'Mum? Are you still watching this?'

'It's boring. Let's switch it off, Love.'

'You were telling me about when Dad got crabs.'

'Ooh. Did he? Been to Cromer, had he?'

Bloody hell! It was getting hard to keep up with her changes in clarity. A thought suddenly hit Elizabeth, as she looked at the dull light in the room. One that she was amazed had never occurred to her before,

'Mum, I know you said you wanted privacy from the street when we made your bed up in here, but it should be in the front room. You'll get the evening sun and see the pansies in your window box.'

Her mother smiled and reached out for her tea, blowing a gentle kiss to her treasured daughter as she nestled back into her pillows.

'I'll move things about tomorrow. Maybe ask Bob to come and give me a hand. I don't know why I didn't think of it before,' Elizabeth smiled as she drew the curtains on the night.

CROSSING BORDERS

*B*ob and Fiona had talked of the trip to Northumberland many times and now, at last, in honour of their twenty-fifth wedding anniversary, they had reached their goal. Bob beamed almost as wide as the wall had once been,

'I knew it would be worth the trip here, but this is something else, int it?'

Before them, the Roman wall was more preserved in this part than Bob had ever dared believe. Expecting only tumbled historic stone in need of a well-read imagination to recreate, he found himself easily transformed to stand as Robert the Bruce, who he had always felt oddly at kin with. Bob's hair was as dark as many Celts but its unusual red highlights, striped clearer in good sun, stood him apart.

'It's so bonnie,' Fiona smiled as she joined her husband's viewing point.

'I wonder how far we can walk it, till it disappears to nothing?' Bob marvelled.

'Well, we've three days to find out, haven't we? So, no need to try and fit something daft in our first day! I ken you… now you've got your proper walking boots.'

Bob planted a kiss on Fiona's cheek and squeezed her hand affectionately, as he had for most of their days over the last twenty-five years. Impressed that there could be no better place to celebrate their anniversary, he let his eyes take in Scotland from the English side of Hadrian's Wall,

'I'd fight for it, wouldn't you? I'm surprised you never came here before now. You weren't so far from it really.'

'Och, I dunnee know about that, Hen. Edinburgh is still two hours or so in a car. You forget we dinnee have a car growing up. And you'd fight for pretty much anything! The Fen Tiger in you stirs at the least sign of confrontation, doesn't it, my pussy cat!' Her playful ribbing and cheeky smile let Bob take it from her with good grace and not react as he would if it was spoken by anyone else. Fiona was his tamer, and he knew she accepted this readily.

'Let's check the information hut out and then plan which way to go.' Stepping down from the raised boulder, Fiona began to search her bag for change, 'It's bound to cost a penny. Is it National Trust or the other one?'

'National Trust covers Scotland too, don't it? Wouldn't seem right for it to be owned by English Heritage some-how, Fi.'

'Well, the bloody Romans were invaders anyway. Shouldn't we get the Italians to pay for its upkeep?' Fiona's laugh was hearty. Bob loved it almost the most of all the things he adored in his woman. It suited her enormous red hair; untamable and yet softly falling on her round face. Her laugh sounded like it was made in her belly and erupted when too full to store anymore. It was contagious and he grinned as he thought on her idea,

'You reckon they would! I can imagine the expressions if it were raised in debate. But there should be something to mark the power of the Scots. Imagine such an immense army shying from them.'

'As much chance of that as seeing the English take the chains off the unicorn,' was Fiona's astute and sharp reply.

A short distance from them, a couple were waiting by the door of the small visitors hut. They could see, as they approached, that the space inside the room was limited and the volunteer fractious.

'Makes you nervous to go in there, don't it?' Bob said under his breath to the guy in front.

'Yes, he's an odd chap. Seems very officious for such a lowly position,' the man responded. He was no taller than Bob but somehow looked 'more'. It was a curious occurrence that Bob had often noted in his life, feeling smaller than someone who was actually a similar size. 'We've been waiting to go in for a good five minutes, but he seems intent on giving those two a grilling. They probably only want a guidebook! If I knew the area better, we'd go on without one, but I don't want to take the less fruitful path.'

The man's posh voice and choice of words left Bob happy to leave it at that, but Fiona and the man's partner had started comparing scarves and Fiona was midsentence on explaining the history of her Celtic knot brooch.

'Great! That will be how we spend this afternoon, no doubt!' The man showed little affection, realising a shopping trip was looming.

'Are you staying nearby or just here for the day?' Bob asked companionably.

'This is the first day of a week's vacation. A well-earned break. And yourself?'

Bob pointed towards the dell they had walked through to reach this point, 'Beyond that, by about a mile, there's a B&B called 'The Walker's Rest'. It caught my wife's eye as we browsed on the internet, 'I'll be needing that' she'd said, not checking into it that much more!'

'How have you found it?'

'Oh, no complaints. We got lucky with it. Only got here last night, 'cause we couldn't leave till I'd got in from work. It's a fair old drive here from The Fens.'

'Oh! That's where you're from. I was trying to detect your accent. Thought it was maybe nearer London. We've travelled a fair way to get here too. Monmouth. Look, Sylvia darling. It's our turn,' he threw a fake scared grin over his shoulder, as he guided his wife into the guardian of the wall's den.

'She seemed nice. We were saying the guy in the hut should have been a traffic warden, but we might have been quick to judge,' Fiona observed, as the grumbling couple retreating from the hut spoke rapidly in their own language with much demonstrative arm throwing, 'I guess he's got his work cut out with some tourists. I have a feeling the guy you were talking to will be fun for him too, ken what I mean?'

This whole encounter had somehow rather soiled Bob's experience of reaching this long-awaited landmark. He felt an anger build in him that was more than mere annoyance, but he was never able to appreciate where it truly stemmed from. Recognising its familiar presence, he closed his eyes and slowly retracted his fingers towards their palms, rhythmically; rather like a cat paws at its mother's belly whilst feeding. With breath slowed and fight-or-flight lessened, he reached out for his wife's reassuring hand and prevented his empathy for the hut employee being carried with him for the rest of the day. Having to be talked down to and to feel worthless was a feeling he knew all too well and he could detect this pain in others in a flash.

※※※

THE PUB WAS PERFECTLY SITUATED for walkers of the wall to reach with heightened appetite and thirst from their last possible stop. Entering it, visitors' eyes needed to make sharp adjustment to the change in light. Such a good, bright day gave a moment of complete blindness to Bob and Fiona, who wavered in the doorway taken by surprise,

'God. Scary, isn't it. Do you think this is what it's like to be blind? I feel a right prat! Do you think everyone's sat staring at us?' He reached to touch Fiona as he spoke, checking her familiarity.

'Oh, Bob! It must take everyone a wee moment to adjust,' as usual his wife's matter-of -fact response calmed his own automatic sensory alarm.

'You get a table while I sort the drinks,' Bob nodded over to the only available space in the full room, 'Maybe they have more room round the back?'

But as Fiona struggled through tight chairs to secure their spot, a man reached the same space on his return from the Gents' and thumped himself heavily down, in claim of the small wooden table. Seeing there was no further room, Fiona scanned the tables discerningly for signs of departure. Lifting her stare, on reluctant admission to a vacation being unlikely for some time, Sylvia from earlier in the day caught her eye. Smiling back, Fiona obeyed her wave to join them, observing that they already shared their table with another couple.

'There's easily room on here for two more, isn't there Frank?'

Sylvia's husband, knowing a rhetorical question, nodded to accommodate his wife explaining that, having arrived at the same time as the other couple, it had been preferable to share rather than waiting indefinitely.

'We can see you're in the same predicament. Fiona, wasn't it? This is my husband, Frank.'

'Hello,' Fiona took each person's handshake whilst introducing Bob on his joining them. The other couple's introduction was followed so purposely by the fact they were both GP's, it almost seemed to be part of their name.

Good at making the most of things, Bob rose to the challenge smiling as appropriate and taking Fiona's hand under the table when breaking between courses. He omitted to partake in the automatic disclosure of profession but, on being asked, found their companions had no questions relating to the brick-laying trade. The understood squeezing code that Fiona and Bob employed gave their unspoken opinion on some of the conversations they were having to partake in but, towards the end of the meal, Bob grew bored with the tedium of the pretence. He would never have to have anything to do with these people ever again, and this evening was too precious to them, as a couple, to be wasted.

He had detected disdain in Frank's tone on hearing they had met whilst on a counselling course and was sure the other woman's condescending remarks were always pointed his way. He had been grateful when Fiona had stepped in so readily with the lie, rather than offer the truth with all its complications. In reality, she had been his counsellor and had to leave it sometime before she devised a 'natural' route to re-find him and declare her interest. He hadn't believed his luck. He had loved her from the first moment he sat with her.

'So, you teach at Monmouth Boys' you say?' The GP from Leicester had looked impressed at Frank's earlier disclosure, and now took it as a lead for his next 'sharing fact', 'We're very fortunate to have such a one-off excellent State school where we are, but it's so hard to get a child in.'

'People move into catchment just for the school but that doesn't always work. We've sacrificed Mikab to get the twins in on the back of him.' The GP's wife's added explanation was so matter of fact that Bob thought he must have taken his eye off the ball for a moment too long and missed some of the conversation. Were they talking about a dog or something?

'Who's Mikab?'

'Our eldest,' the woman had gawped, finishing her mouthful of dessert before continuing, 'It's the only way.'

'How d'ya mean, 'sacrified'?' Fiona added, equally flummoxed.

'Oh, I know the term,' Frank interjected. 'He'll board. To get the others in too. Will your twins have to board?'

'No, thank God! Costly business, bringing up children. Especially when you get three instead of the intended two!' The male GP laughed. 'You've only recently reduced your hours haven't you, Aanya? You'd be needing to go full-time again!'

'Do you work at the same practice?' Frank's wife continued the conversation with what looked like genuine interest, but Bob squeezed Fiona's hand so sharply it made her jump. The signal was understood, and she looked to her watch in classily smooth response,

'Where's the time go? Bob, we need to be back. We dinnee take a key because we said we'd be back by ten.'

'Yes, Love. We must be off. Pleasure to meet you all. Happy walking.'

'Happy Anniversary again,' a couple of them chorused together, raising a further glass in honour of the already vanishing pair.

'Let's just pay as fast as we can and get out of here,' Bob whispered as his nod got the barman's attention,

'Just for ours, please. We're paying separately,' and to Fiona, 'It will be good to get outside again. Feel the air.'

The heat in the packed room had joined the low ceiling in becoming oppressive and tomb-like. Bob wanted nothing more than space and quiet and his Fiona next to him as they strode the miles back to their unassuming B&B.

※※※

'You've been quiet these last two days, Love. I ken, something's on your mind,' Fiona hadn't wanted to interrupt his reflections as they walked, taking in the rugged beauty around them that, for herself, had filled her being and stolen any room for distractions. But, after twenty-five years of close living she could read her husband's moods almost entirely. He was sinking into a place that was dark and painful for him, she could tell. She imagined its complex structure peeling like a further layer of wallpaper but not yet showing the design on the layer below it and the hint at yet so many more beyond would, she knew, create a freeze point in Bob.

Now, as they headed towards home after a short stop at Wetherby, she turned to watch his expression as he drove, 'Dunnee eye-roll and shove your weight like you can throw me off. You need to talk about it, Love. It can't be ignored when it's so much a part of you.'

'You know as much as I do, don't you? I've shared everything with you, Fiona. You seem to understand me better than I know myself.'

'You know I'm here, Pet.' Fiona said, after a moment's reflection; her outstretched arm touching his leg reassuringly. His thigh felt more muscular than she could ever remember. It must be all the manual work he'd been doing, with more people than ever wanting extensions and the like.

Understanding that Bob would talk once ready, she let the matter go. She had a feeling it would raise itself again before too long. It seemed closer than ever before.

It wasn't long after leaving Wetherby that they drove past a hitch-hiking couple looking forlorn. The woman raised her thumb with some determination, but the chap looked frazzled, as if about to fall.

'Do you think he's on something?' Fiona glanced back, as they passed a road sign telling of the miles to Newark, 'Bob?'

Seeing Bob was lost in consideration of the information she knew he'd be amassing from their hurried glance; she wasn't so much as surprised as sceptical when he announced, 'I think I'll pull in, see if they clock we're waiting for them.'

'Oh, Bob. That's so like you. But he's no damaged bird. He could be drugged up to his eyeballs.'

'There's something about him. They'll have a story, and it will give the next part of our journey an interest, won't it?'

Fiona pulled a doubtful face and picked at some fluff blown round the car from the open window,

'Look at that, Bob! It looks more like fur than fluff. Like cat fur. You'd think we had a ginger Tom in the back!'

⁂

'You didn't think you'd be helped, Mate, did you?' Bob laughed to the younger man, as he climbed in the back, having trampled on his ciggie, 'I could see it in your expression. And I suppose it's not just the hitch-hiking that's got you that way.'

The man coughed into his hand and nodded to signal he'd heard the comment but gave nothing more. He looked so uncomfortable. Was it his own skin he recoiled from? Bob felt moved by the similarity. He would have eagerly shed his skin like a selkie when he was that age.

'We didn't think we'd get a ride the whole stretch to Sutton Bridge, that's for sure,' his more able other half laughed, 'Felt sure we'd be walking again after the A1.'

'Aye. It's a coincidence we're not that far from Norwich ourselves. I'm Fiona and this is Bob. We've been to Hadrian's Wall for a few days, how aboot yourselves?'

There was a moment of quiet, a weighted hush, a pause that threatened to implode with its content. Fiona, good at listening, waited happily but Bob not bearing the tension of the unspoken chirped,

'Let them be, Fiona. You can see they must have got themselves in a pickle. Not running from the law, are you?' His attempt to cheer them only created more mystery, as Bob caught the woman dabbing her eyes as she looked out her window.

'We went to Scotland in my camper, but she broke down. It's too much money to fix her up so we ditched her and are getting back thumbing it instead.' The man's explanation gave no emotion only fact, clearly leaving any further detail curtailed, and instead he took the conversation to The Fens, 'I've got family somewhere near Sutton Bridge. Mentioned them on the way down here, didn't I, Clare,' he informed his woman.

'Bet we know them then. It's a small place. What's their name?'

'Dunno. Had nothing to do with them. It was my grandad's lot.'

'You'll have the same surname if it's on your dad's side,' pressed Bob, excited that there could be a connection, but his hitch hiker's eyes had glazed over and his expression clearly left the conversation.

'That rain's falling hard now, int it, Love? Wet old August, this one,' Fiona threw in. 'I like when the rain falls on a slant like this. Seems to soften the horizontal Fen lines.

When I first moved down, I cunnae believe badgers could live here, could I, Bob? Remember that? We'd pass a dead one on the road and I'd say, 'how can that live here? There's nowhere for it to hide its sett.' No woods or bank. But then you get to appreciate the land better.'

Bob nodded his recall of these conversations but digressed, always interested to air history, to speak with passion and knowledge as the arterial A17 continued through its bleak agricultural scene, 'I'm reading about the old Roman roads just now. Visiting Hadrian's Wall has really whet my appetite. There's so many legacies they've left us to discover.'

'Was this a Roman road then?' the woman asked, seemingly recovered from her earlier emotional frailty.

'No, I don't think so. No one disturbed the Fens too much before the 1600's. But there're major roads right near here, like the one from York to London…that goes through Lincoln. Lincoln would have been a really major place.' Noting the woman at least seemed interested, Bob continued, happy to impart some knowledge from his love of books, 'I've read a lot about how The Fens once were. Destroyed in the name of improvement but, in truth, just to line the rich pigs' pockets. As Fen Tigers, we fought decade upon decade, tooth and nail, to keep these lands as they were, deterring the enemy for up to a hundred years at a time. You'd have been Tigers, just like me. So successful we were in our tactics, that we defied the greed of those wanting to destroy our marshes for centuries.'

'What they want them for?' The woman's voice hid scorn in its doubt, revealing a possible contempt for her homeland.

'They figured if they drained the Fens, it would be great agricultural land; which was true. Only thing was, a handful of the wealthiest landowners claimed they owned it all. Ignored the fact thousands of fen folk lived on the land; their livelihood was the nature of the marsh. So, we battled and battled, sabotaging all their efforts, wasting their money and time.'

'Well, they must have won in the end, 'cause there ain't no marshes round here no more,' came a coarse line from the young man, who noticeably twitched, desperate to light another cigarette.

'They still struggle to control it. If left alone, it would soon revert to marsh. I think the Tigers' spirit lives on,' said Bob, hoping his words would fall like a much-needed seed to implant hope in an obviously barren soil. He brushed his hand over his mouth, as a cat cleans its face, as he returned to concentrate on his driving once more.

A SNARLING COMING from the bathroom woke Fiona up sharp, like an alert sentry, from her deep sleep. Feeling Bob was out of the bed, she knew it must be him, but the noise was so odd she couldn't be sure what it actually was. As she called his name it converted into a sob and she ran to the closed door now fully awake,

'Let me in, Love. Let me in.'

One look at his tormented face, with eyes wet and tired from many tears, she had no need of 'what is it?' or an attempt to console, to lessen his exceptional outpour. She simply placed her hand on his to let him know she was there and, after some minutes had passed, she gingerly asked, as she sat next to him on the side of the bathtub,

'What do you think stirred it up?'

'It's so many things, Fi. That guy Frank for one, with his stiff superiority and their conversation about 'sacrificing' your kids? Like, what's with them? It's like they see kids as a commodity, to be used in their game of life.'

'I knew that would stir you, Love. I hate to hear that talk too. You ken I do. But they're just different to us, that's all. I suppose they love their bairns the same as another, but life is a lot more about promoting yourselves to them.'

'Like the flippin' capitalists that stole our marshes,' Bob glared as he grabbed at more loo roll, blowing his nose like a snarl. 'Leaving half-men, full of anger and resentment... like that Shaun we gave the lift to. Talk about a lost soul,' he continued, louder, as he stalked back to the bedroom,

'It's clearly written on their faces, but no one cares to look. It's like it's only visible if you know the same pain. And I keep seeing it, being aware of it, Fiona. It's all around and I'm sick of the taste of it, the feeling in my stomach, the cloud that won't leave me. It's so oppressive. The waiting. Always a waiting. When I was a kid, it was like I was sewn into the land and we waited for the weather as one...the clouds to break or the rain to give over, an' I still feel it now. Or the waiting to be accepted; chosen for footie or for a part in a play,' his passion had become a rant, emotion over-riding care and awareness. He'd become the tiger; blazing, bursting through the flames that controlled him, roaring at the boundaries he'd been confined in, furious at the years he'd been captive,

'I thought I'd broken through it when mum told me I was adopted. When I could fit that bit of my oddness into the puzzle after twenty years of not knowing. But it broke me down, instead of building me up. You know the mess I was in when I first met you. And then, I felt complete for a long while once we were together. But it's never enough, is it Fi? I can't fill it…the hunger. The hole. Twenty-five good years we've been married but I'm still not complete.'

'The things that you've heard and seen lately have started you thinking. They're threads of thoughts that come from the centre of things. Try and face it, Love. What is it, Bob? What's the hole?'

'I thought maybe if we could have had kids. If we could have filled all the quieter moments, the spaces in time, but that wouldn't have fixed it, would it, Fi?' With his head buried in his hands, it was harder to distinguish each word that ran so eagerly into the next. Fiona felt an urge to stroke him. He looked so strokable, with his hair rumpled and dishevelled in his mad mane sort of way.

'I know it's something in me that I have to find for myself,' he continued. 'I need to accept 'me' better and stop hiding from the thing that's lurked over my head and tapped on my shoulder for what feels like all of my life.'

He stood by the bed. Looking suddenly cub-like. It was clear he didn't know what to do with himself, whether to collapse in more tears or to pace the room angrily. It was easy to imagine him as the small boy he once was. Maybe getting out of bed to change his PJ's; Fiona instinctively knew he would have wet the bed.

'I need to know them, Fi. I need to find my own family. To know who I am.'

'Of course, you do, Pet.' Keeping her reply simple, to provide all the support and encouragement required, she patted her side to encourage his seat, 'It feels like the right time now then, Hen?'

'I'm fifty, for God's sakes. It's now or never. With Mum passed, I think I feel ready. Less disloyal.'

'Oh, I think Ruby would have helped you, Bob. I'm sure you'd have had her blessing, tough as she might have thrown it! You know I'll help you. We'll make this journey together and see where crossing your border takes us, shall we? They'll be no fight needed. You can put away your claws.'

SHADOW OF SHAME

*L*ooking back, it had started on a Sunday. A bright spring morning with the smell of narcissus wafting from reception and the usual drab hallway lit attractively by a shaft of light through its entrance's fanlight.

The South Brink Hotel wasn't posh by today's standards. In fact, it may have only achieved a maximum of three stars in any TripAdvisor ratings, but this was some years ago. TripAdvisor didn't exist and posh was a Viennetta dessert or an After Eight with your coffee. The hotel supplied both, and I, the teenage receptionist on Sunday afternoons, would sneakily pocket handfuls of the chocolate mints and gorge on them whilst swinging idly in the chair at the desk.

I was offered extra hours to waitress on Sunday dinners. Again, this was before the publics' contemporary interest in food; well before Vegan was a common word and a Vegetarian was to be treated very suspiciously indeed. Lord knows what the options were, but I should think it was to take the meat off the plate and have the rest as your roast dinner.

There was a trainee chef, Sonia, in the kitchen shadowing Stuart, the guy whose hair looked as if it stored the deep-fat fryer's oil and whose belly could be containing all the bar's beer. I couldn't believe he had a qualification in cooking, as the evidence strongly suggested otherwise, but he regularly boasted that he had daily fed four hundred men in the Army so maybe he'd just grown lazy in the comparative ease of his current role.

Sonia seemed friendly, not so much older than me, and we got to chatting when we shared a fag break together. Now, I might have to explain that then, a fag was a cigarette. It hadn't been nicked to be of any other interpretation, as far as I'm aware. And 'nicked' is a word we all used in Wisbech.

Sonia had two little children but was a single mum. Their dad, who sounded like a bit of a waster, had them when she worked and only her boy was old enough for school. I'd thought she was younger than her twenty-four years and when she smiled her youth was more pronounced, making her seem more like an oversized ten-year-old. Her laugh was childlike too and I liked that she got my silly humour and seemed to appreciate my company.

I said I could babysit if she ever wanted and, although she laughed saying she never really went out, her eyes seemed to brighten at the possibility. I think it was only a couple of weeks later that she asked if I could. I was upstairs, chambermaiding (yes, the receptionist had a variety of roles). It must have been a Saturday morning because she apologised for the short notice but wondered if I could help her out that evening. She couldn't ask Dave (her ex) as he'd get silly about her having a date. It was nothing serious…just 'going out'. Probably come to nothing anyway, she gestured with her shrugged shoulders and scrunched face.

She was renting a semi-detached house down the Old Lynn Road. I hadn't been in any houses along there before, although I'd often passed them on the way to my friends. They were neither big nor small and inside hers it was quite basic and didn't feel all that homely yet. I knew she'd just started renting it and that there's not much point in spending anything on someone else's property. There were toys here and there and everything you needed, like a sofa, TV, table and chairs. I was excited for when I could move out and have a place of my own, in just a couple of years' time. My mum always said 'wait till you're eighteen' but I felt ready for it then. As soon as school was done in a couple of months' time, I'd move out. But really, I wasn't a fully prepared fledgling; still pretty naïve about lots of things, although I doubt I would have acknowledged that then.

Both the children were already settled in bed and even an hour in I felt bored and restless. With only three TV channels and no mobile phone or laptops, there were limited things to do. There were no books, and the only magazine was a Beano. Having made myself a cup of tea and eaten most of the packet of biscuits left for me, I went for a nosey. Come on, really? Isn't it what every babysitter does? I like knowing where I am, to become familiar with my surroundings. And, anyway, who really would care? I was only interested to see the layout.

I didn't widen the children's door but poked my head in enough to see that both were soundly sleeping and tussled in the covers as really only kids do. Their limbs cross ways and hanging limply over the sides rather than contained by the bed in any sort of way. A sweet sweaty odour claimed the room as their own.

There were four more doors, one to the bathroom, another to an airing cupboard and the two remaining, bedrooms. In the largest one, which was well lit from the street lighting outside, I stepped in a little to see Sonia's work uniform thrown over a chair. Messy make-up spread over the carpet at the foot of a standing mirror. But the dominant things in the sparsely decorated room were the dark wooden bed and wardrobe.

As I came a little further in, to watch the busy road from the window, an unexpected noise caught my attention. It seemed to be coming from the far-right corner of the room where the wardrobe was. Yes. It was definitely coming from inside the wardrobe. It was as if there was something in the bottom corner, maybe scampering about. I strained my ears to try and decipher what it sounded like but the nearest I could get was like a rustling. Not loud or particularly frantic but some sort of movement of paper. Or was it scratching? I puzzled it for a moment more but never considered getting any closer or actually taking a peek. It seemed like a really odd place to keep something like a pet, perhaps. Would a caged bird make that sound or a hamster? I certainly didn't dare look. What if it escaped and Sonia would know that I had been sneaking about?

I didn't think too much about it until Sonia asked me if I could sit again a week later. I had popped into the hotel to say hello on my way home from school. Being a short walk from our house and backing onto the road that my school was on, it was good to sometimes grab a cup of tea and chat with whoever was free. And there was always someone free because the hotel was seldom that busy.

Sonia had seemed agitated and told me her son was in trouble with school again. She was proper bothered by it, so when she asked about the babysitting, I felt it would be good for her. I had nothing planned and the money was handy, of course, but I felt a bit of trepidation, after last time, on approaching the ordinary-looking house once more. I'd just make sure I didn't go near her mysterious wardrobe.

As it was earlier in the evening this time, I got to play with the children a little before settling them to bed. It wasn't till later, when again I was bored with the pathetic offerings on her TV, that I noticed a large crack in the ceiling. It came from the corner of the room but oddly ran diagonally across the ceiling rather than edging horizontally close to the wall. I wondered if I just hadn't noticed it before.

I babysat a few more times after that, each time noticing that the ceiling's crack was getting larger and deeper. I mentioned it to Sonia when she came home, and she laughed it off saying the landlord wouldn't care if the ceiling fell in. He wasn't bothered about anything but getting his rent.

Each shift at the hotel, I noticed a change in Sonia's demeanour. She wasn't quite so chatty and told me several times of how much trouble her children were getting in. Her three-year-old was biting and the one at school stealing from other kids. She told me how their dad did nothing with them when they were at his, and that they watched endless TV while he smoked weed and drank with his mates. She thought maybe they were trying to get attention. She told me how she wanted them to have a different life from hers, but I wasn't sure what she meant by 'different'. Expectations were lower in the seventies and eighties. You put up with what you got and that was pretty much it.

She was dating a different guy now, as the previous one was 'a right wanker'. I took a book along with me on this occasion, knowing that by eight, the children wouldn't be around for company. I was babysitting at least once a week now, but I didn't mind; the tenners added up. Looking at her broken ceiling I noticed that more and more cracks were branching off the original, deep one. It created the look of a sparse tree. It seemed oddly starving. And it was clear that it all started from this one particular corner. I was curious to work out which room was above the sitting room and quickly calculated it had to be Sonia's bedroom as it also faced onto the road. So, what was above this exact area of ceiling? What was in the right-hand corner of Sonia's bedroom? Oh God. I knew instantly, could recall seeing the room's lay-out. It was the bloody, scratching wardrobe, wasn't it?

I can't tell you how wobbly I felt putting my hand on the doorknob and peeping round into her bedroom again. Why I felt I needed to look seems incredible to me now. I must have just been more adventurous and thought myself invincible because I know, for sure, you wouldn't catch me investigating a curiosity like that these days. What was most weird about it was that, from the other side of the door, the room had appeared quiet but once past the threshold there was a really loud shuffling of what seemed like paper coming from the wardrobe. Whatever it was, it created enough force to be rocking it slightly and hitting it occasionally against the wall. Was someone in there? What the hell was going on? I backed out, through the door, just as swiftly as I had glanced in; as soon as I'd registered that the wardrobe moved and banged, I was out of there. Leaning briefly against her bedroom door, panting in the corridor, I wasn't sure I could conquer my natural flight instinct. The best my terrified brain could do was instruct me to get into the children's bedroom and wait there, with them...for what? Wait. What a bloody awful word in this scenario. Waiting was terrifying. My frozen thought process was as useless to me as my failure to physically function.

As I watched the children sleep, with only an occasional fidget or restless stirring to dissolve once more into blissful unawareness, the house was silent. It was as if I had created the bizarre scenario in my head and was the only one able to observe it. I decided I would ask Sonia about the cracks; that I'd make out that I had heard banging whilst downstairs in the sitting room. Yeh; looked up, seen the huge crack and been worried. So, checking it out, had seen the wardrobe move. Had heard noise coming directly from it. I swore there was no way I was going to babysit there again. I stayed curled beneath the window, amongst their littered floor of sharp Duplo bricks and sticky sweet wrappers, until I heard Sonia's key in the lock.

She had come home a bit worse for wear and I reckoned it was a good time to ask, as she would maybe not remember I had in the morning. She didn't even register surprise that I was looking quite shaken and had raced down the stairs quite loudly by the time she had bent to pull her shoes off. Her eyes had been swimming with the alcohol but became sharply focused, like an eagle locked on prey, when I said I thought there might be something in her wardrobe. Her pupils looked to shrink back into her head.

'Did you look?' Any anger or threat contained seemed to be directed only at herself, so her question sounded panicked and scared more than anything.

'What is it? Why can't you let whatever it is out?'

·☆☆·

EASTER CAME a bit later that year, so was mid-April. I was waitressing on the Sunday and Sonia was the only cook, as

Stuart was off sick. We did have half the hotel full and a couple of non-residents dining, but I had seen it busier at Christmas and thought it was all in hand. Sonia was swearing and banging, though, and there was a tension building that felt really uncomfortable. Richard, the owner, popped in and out to help but his permed wife, with nails like polished talons, never made an entrance. We only knew she existed because we saw her driving out of the carpark in her MG some days.

I had hardly seen Sonia since I'd last babysat but didn't want her to think I was distancing myself from the weird wardrobe 'conversation'. It had just been discarded, but not far enough that it couldn't now hover over us, and it persisted grimly and begged for attention. Now, I noticed, she had a bit less time for me and seemed quite fragile. When the shift was done and the last of the plates were out of the dishwasher, I asked her if something was wrong.

'Only that twat,' she spat bitterly, indicating the door that Richard had left through a little earlier. 'He needs to learn to keep his hands to himself. I hate that men think they can do that to me.'

'What? Has he touched you?' I asked with immediate fury and unquestioning sisterly support.

'He's always doing it. Pushing me to walls and pressing into me. Sticking his tongue down my throat.'

'Bloody hell. Can't you tell him you'll tell his wife or something?'

'I need this job and going from one to the other every few months don't look good, does it. Like he's bothered by anything I can say. He'll just deny it and say I've made it up. Or that it's me coming on to him. I know how it works.'

I didn't know what to say. I could see all her points and it did feel quite hopeless. She seemed so angry and yet almost resigned to that sort of behaviour.

'Shall I come over tonight, with a bottle of wine? We could rent a video if your player works. Here…' I said cheekily popping a white from the fridge into my bag that hung ready on the back of the door, 'He owes you that much.' I didn't mind going to her house if she was there too, and maybe she'd talk to me about the secret she hid in her bedroom.

At first, I thought Sonia's front room was just dark because the light wasn't yet switched on but once it was, there was still an awful shadow cast over the space. The cracks had come right down the walls, branching in all directions from the ceiling but, when you studied them minutely, it was clear that they all still came from a main one, stemming from the top right-hand corner. Like the trunk. Or the artery. That was the dark, black heart to this tangled beast of a problem. Surely now Sonia would get the landlord in?

'Doesn't it bother you?' I asked incredulously, 'I find it really spooky.'

She had just looked at me, with her wide eyes which I suddenly realised were so tired. No longer holding the sparkle of a ten-year-old, but with the weight of all time.

'I could show you something. But it's really hard for me to do.' Her words were staggered, and she bit her nails and pulled at her face in-between the deliverance, 'But I've got a feeling you won't tell anyone.'

I read the instruction in her check for confirmation, 'You're right. I won't. Whatever it is.' Whatever it was, I knew it must be containable; something she had a relation-ship with. She was living with it here all the time. She wouldn't be putting her kids at risk, surely? Maybe I had just let my mind run away with itself, with my over-active imagination.

As she walked in front of me, up the stairs and slowly along the skinny corridor to her room, her own anguish was clearly visible and magnified that of my own. What on earth was I doing? I felt nauseous and pathetically weak. I felt myself physically pull away from the approaching room and yet mentally pressured myself on. My heart was fluttering like a bird's. It felt too light and fast to pull through its anxiety and I wondered if I might pass out.

I could sense the magnitude of the occasion, as Sonia stepped closer still to the now-rocking wardrobe. It was stomping and crashing back down, throwing weight round in a way that made no sense. As if it would hurl itself deliberately at her and yet she stoically remained at her task. If a man was contained in there, he was a lunatic. If he got out, surely we would be dead? Why hadn't we heard this thrashing of such a heavy wooden weight while coming up the stairs, when outside her room? How were the children sleeping through it?

Miraculously, and so instantly that it defied any logic at all, the wardrobe returned to that of an inanimate object the second Sonia tore its door open. Inside clothes had remained on their hangers, shoes were paired on the bottom shelf, and there was no hint at all of any distur-bance. More surprising still, nothing…not of gigantic ogre proportion or even the faintest hint of feather sprang free from its containment. There appeared to be nothing at all unruly let alone something threatening.

Sonia had scooped down to collect a shoe box from the right-hand corner of the wardrobe floor. Once my shaking seemed manageable and the jittery shallow breaths could be replaced with something more substantial, I asked her what the box contained whilst watching her spill the papers out onto her bed. There were official stamps on lots of the sheets and the headed paper was the same on most. Social Services. Report after report from Social Services. Ranging from twenty-four years before, they came up through the seventies. All had her first name on, although the surnames were different on quite a few. Hospital letters and Court Orders mixed in with the odd drawing or note scribbled in her child-hand from the past.

She sat on the floor, resting her arms on the bed and tucking her head down into its throw. She wouldn't look at me but seemed to want me to know something about her. Something she couldn't use words to express. I moved a few sheets around to get a gist of what story they contained.

'Did you get adopted?'

'Once. Yeh. But they sent me back 'cause of the way I am.' Such shame was expressed in those few words that I remember my eyes had stung, instinctively knowing something about that just wasn't right. It had been painful to look at her expression, her face. Her eyes were dry and expressed no pity or resentment but a clear acceptance to all she had been led to believe; resigned to an unfounded truth.

'How do you mean? How old were you when you were put in Care?'

Her face winced at the word 'Care'. She spoke to the carpet when she replied, 'I was six. I was always being told I was lucky. Being helped before it was too late, and that they'd try to keep me with my little sister. No damage

75

would be done. So, when I grew up causing so many issues, I knew it was me. Cause I'm rotten.'

'Rotten? You? There's nothing wrong with you. Look how you are managing…'

'I'm NOT managing. I'm NOT doing anything right. It's all screwed up,' she wailed. A trail of tears seemed to fall in seconds from the pressure of being fiercely contained for too, too long. I remember feeling panicked because she reminded me a bit of my mum when she got like this. To comfort her in any way might lead to being rebuked and alight a fury, so I kept my distance and shut my mouth for what seemed like an hour.

'Did you all stay together then?' I had ventured timidly.

A head shake, heavy, mournful, resigned, 'Nah. Within a few months we were split up. None of us stayed together.'

'I'm sorry,' but hearing it fall from me like an inadequate brick of a word, left awkward silence once more. 'Do you get any support from Social Services now? With your own kids?'

She lifted her eyes to mine to show such contempt at my words that I again swallowed hard, feeling totally out of my depth.

'Social Services don't bloody support. That's not what they do. They take in fragile and vulnerable kids and hard-boil them, so they're less likely to crack. They monitor and record-keep, handing kids out and bringing them back in and there's no bloody way they're going to do that with mine.' She blew her nose so ferociously, it seemed she was trying to blow her anger out.

'But I don't get it. Why this rocks the wardrobe. How it can?' I asked naively.

'It's not sound is it. I'm not sound,' was all she whimpered in explanation.

⁂

I WOULD LIKE to say that it was me who helped her find her feet, work through her shame, and throw away her baggage. But it wasn't. I was out of there as fast as I could be, aware that I was totally out of my depth and with no experience to offer. If our lives had been put on scales, to measure the weight of pain we each carried, Sonia would have shot me off my lightweight end. But that's not to say she was forgotten to me, that her situation didn't play on my mind, stay on my conscience, and often revisit my memories over the years.

I only saw her one more time at work, because she handed in her notice and told me she had got a job at a hair salon in town. She explained that because it was run by a woman with mostly women clients; men shouldn't be able to invade her space there and take it away from her. She had decided to put her youngest into playschool in the mornings and set up a childminder to collect her for the afternoons. She could apply for money for childcare that she hadn't known she could and that would make a big difference on her reliance on their skunk of a dad. There was something a bit more illuminated about her; maybe sharing her secret, her mis-placed shame, had opened possibilities for her? I didn't know how that could really be, but a change was apparent.

When I bumped into her next it was seven years later, and I took a moment to be sure it was her. I was back for a very rare weekend visiting my parents, having left Wisbech five years earlier to start a course in journalism. Sonia looked fashionable and happy as she ran joyfully to me from the other side of the road.

'Hey you. Long time, no see!'

'You look so different!' I had laughed, admiring her red belt. 'I think it's your hair. It really suits you like that. Do you still work at Sally's?' I felt awkward as soon as I'd spoken it, realising how it was almost improbable that she could have stuck to one job for so long.

'Yeh. Sal's great. She's just what I needed. You'll never believe what...' her face beamed. It was fantastic to witness the change that had come over her. 'I want you to see, rather than tell you. It was so bloody amazing. I'm now on my way home, have you got time to pop in a minute to see?'

I was surprised that she was still renting the same house and felt the same nervous anxiety from those younger years on entering her doorway. I guessed she'd have insisted it was re-plastered by now, and have added more soul to the place perhaps. And sure enough, when led into the sitting room by her excitedly shaking hand, the cracks were nowhere to be seen.

'The landlord sorted it out then?' I laughed.

'No. I did! It was never a fault with the plaster.' Her voice sounded proudly delirious, and she let her story spill with eager excitement, 'I'll explain...it was so weird. And you'll maybe think I'm making it up because it was SO weird. But, every time I put a foot in the right direction, reached out for help or stopped myself from doing stuff that would do me no good, a crack would disappear. It was like, I dunno...if I was kind to myself, I'd heal a crack! Is that too impossible? But it's honestly what happened till, eventually, it was a clear, intact ceiling again.

'The night I showed you my box of papers, I came down here after you'd left. I couldn't sleep and was in a right mess. It had been SUCH a big step for me, telling you who I really was. What I thought I really was. Voicing my shame. The cracks had gone AWOL…like a flippin' web. They had spread over the walls so bad it felt like they were moving, had a pulse. I was really scared. Thought I was going mental. I curled up in the chair, shaking and nearly threw up with the terrible fear and panic that was overwhelming me. Then suddenly…you might not believe this, but it's true…'

I nodded in encouragement, doubting I would ever think anything was impossible again having shared her peculiar wardrobe experience.

'I smelt this familiar perfume quite strongly. I couldn't place it for a while, and I was struggling to concentrate on where the memory was from; what the perfume was linked to. But then it came, like a flash. It was the scent of a foster woman I'd known, called Ruby. Hers had been the first place we were taken to, the night they removed us. We'd all been there together for a few months, and it felt OK. I remembered she would hold me close and stroke my hair while she read me story after story. She was really comforting and so was her smell. I must have eventually slept, thinking about that, with the perfume over me like a blanket. When I woke, it felt different. Weird. Like after a storm. I could see that the main crack from this corner…' she pointed up high at the area I had first seen the cracks develop. '…had gone. Remember? It was so wide, like a trunk, but it had completely disappeared. The rest were still there, all over the place, but not coming from that main one anymore, not feeding from where it had once been.'

'That's crazy weird. God, you must have felt…I don't know…what did you feel?'

'Just bloody fantastic! I felt somehow different but everything around me was just the same. That day, I went to all the chemists, spraying their testers, to find which perfume it was. So, I got a bottle of Anais Anais when I matched it and, with the scent on my skin, felt kind of empowered. Well, it helped me.' She shrugged, recognising the improbability of everything she was disclosing but not doubting its effect.

'It became like a game. I'd do something positive, to change how my life was shaping up, and race back here to see if a crack had gone. They started going from the walls first.' She paused in her revelation, to hold my hand, 'But this is all I really needed to get going.' She raised our hands up to punch the air in solidarity, 'To be held. By the right people. Thank you for starting it off for me.'

I could only smile back. Warmly. Squeeze her hand and, in so doing, was reminded again of how vulnerable we all are; how childlike our hands can feel in each other's. I felt immensely happy that she had changed her destiny and taken back what could have so easily been stolen from her. She had anchored herself. Sally had taken her under her wing, not only giving her an apprenticeship but supporting her like a daughter; helping her join support groups and listening tirelessly to all her stories of abuse and horror, and so dissolving her secret store of hidden shame.

LISA'S LEGACY

2 3rd Sept 1986

I've been thinking about my sister. Sonia. I don't
know what started it, maybe seeing the woman in the park
last week. I don't often give her a thought, to be honest,
but I caught this woman's eyes and we both lingered the
acknowledgment, just for a moment, but a moment too
long; as if enquiring, searching each other's souls. It was
uncanny. I was stopped mid-sentence, with thoughts of
Sonia instantly there: is this what she'll look like in a few
years' time? Cause there was something about the woman's
face that seemed so familiar; the way her head turned half
laughing, before we caught each other's eyes, and brought
the moment to a still. What was she thinking that made her
stop too?

I knew she couldn't be Sonia because she was only two
years older than me, and this lady looked a good ten more.
It didn't even occur to me 'could she be my mother?' as I
never go there. She's not someone I hunger for half as
much as my sister. But, when I got home, and allowed the
memory to replay, I worked out the years and knew it
couldn't have been her, either. It's a funny thing not

knowing who you are part of. Maybe she is related somehow but I don't care to know. No one took us in when we were taken and no one kept us together, so our relatives don't exist.

That stung. I thought the point of this diary is to get healthier in my thinking, not harbour grudges and resentments. When Lorraine first suggested I keep a diary, well, she calls it a journal, I looked at her like 'what? You serious?' I don't have time for all that remembering crap and don't have enough happening most days to even fill a line. But she gently kind of steered me towards it and promised I'll never have to show it so, I don't know, I just kind of started writing. English had been my best subject at school, helped 'cause I loved reading so much maybe? So, I just got into it and the pages began to crowd with things they couldn't contain. My words were like swimming from me and diving into a pool of penetrable dark. Like at the end of a waterfall, hitting the water hard and creating something just by smashing it. But the words could swim, they came back up again and didn't stay deep down without trace because they were searching for light and didn't want to stay submerged anymore.

Lorraine said, 'Search a bit deeper when you write next time', seeing through my initial dishonest entries that I chose to share, eager to demonstrate how carelessly I could throw them at her, with my hard heart beating fast to keep up with my sneered, mocking words. She's been patient with my bad attitude. I don't think she actually judges me 'cause I've said plenty of mean stuff to her, but she still lets me see her. But she'll want me to explore the feelings I've been having since I saw that look-a-like stranger last week, because that's how therapists think.

I last saw Sonia when I was four. I remember one memory of her really clearly. It wasn't long after we'd arrived at the first foster house, and I remember I'd gone straight to sleep. It was nighttime so that was probably why, but I used to sleep through things when it got too hard. Yeh, with the help of sedatives now, but it used to be my natural coping mechanism. I'd woken up after a bit though because it was all so unfamiliar, and a guy I didn't know was standing in the room rocking my baby brother, who was crying his head off. I sneaked downstairs to find Sonia; I remember being scared. I remember the man saying to go downstairs and find Ruby. That was the lady who was looking after us.

I was so quiet; I hardly dared breathe. I sat down in the doorway watching the woman with my sister on her knee. Sonia was cuddled right up into her, tight like a ball, and I only knew it must be her 'cause of her red jumper. The one with stars on the front. They didn't see me because the chair had almost its back to the door. But I could hear Ruby's story and see her gentle stroking of my sister's hair and I wanted badly to go and see the book, join them. But I couldn't. I don't know why, 'cause I know I wanted that hug something awful, I wanted to be with my sister so much: but I couldn't join them. I watched from afar and felt frozen. I didn't cry. I felt so outside of myself. So alone. So, lost.

We stayed at that house together for a while but it's hard to say how long. Not long enough. Moved in the spring, I think, 'cause the birds were making nests and this Ruby had daffodils in her house. I get funny when I see daffodils, even now. Sonia was taken away first. The social workers talked to us a bit about it, but I don't think they ever told me where Sonia was going to live. I just know it wasn't anywhere I could find her.

I don't know who cried more when she had to leave, 'cause Ruby wailed in the kitchen that night once she'd put me to bed. She probably didn't think I could hear her, but I couldn't sleep that night, no matter how much I tried. My survival mechanism failed me, big time; like it was outsmarted. I think I was listening out; sure Sonia would be back. She would have got away from them and would come in at any minute. Wriggling halfway down the bed, so I'd be away from the outside wall which could drag me from the house, I could hear Ruby still sobbing in her room when she came up later. I left a few weeks after that.

25TH SEPT 1986

What a bitch! That cow Sharpe, fucking Spider-Woman, has got it in for me. Ever since the first day introduction. Everyone else volunteering, doing relatable work and being flippin' healthcare assistants and then my turn. Oh yeh! What a surprise. No previous nursing experience. What's to scoff at about bloody packing carrots? It was a job, wasn't it? Just while I was waiting. It was a laugh, too. I loved it. Maybe I'll go back to it; if this stuffy-nosed cow gets her way, I'll have to.

Thank God for Debbie. At least her holiday hotel work helped balance my omission a bit! And then I met Chris in our flat share, and she's only been filling doughnuts in Baker's Oven, for Christ's sakes! Bet she never got so judged on that though.

I'm never going to do well here with that battle-axe Sharpe standing over me. Christ! But she's got the ammunition she was after now; I've had a pretty poor report off our first ward placement. They were a cold bunch if ever there were, and bloody nurses, too. I thought this was a caring profession. It just went on and on about what I don't know and can't do and that my attitude sucks. Strange that, 'cause I know I've had lots of lovely conversations with the patients on that ward. They pull my leg and laugh when I get muddled; much more supportive than any of the staff have been.

But the way Sharpe looked at me, the words she threw to deliberately harm me, how could she be that mean? What's wrong with her? I'm sure she thinks she's got the better of me, but she knows nothing. Is there something about me that makes her jealous? She doesn't look the type to want a man in her life but maybe she can tell I've had a few and it hurts her somehow? Cause I'm young? Got some attitude? Smoke?

Or, maybe, she does know who I am somehow? I don't know how she could 'cause I put nothing about being adopted on my application form. Wasn't relevant, was it? But it does probably show. It's like a burn on my face; a pallor on my skin. I don't look as well-fed or rich or some-thing. I can't think what the word is, but you see the differ-ence in the way posh kids are. The contrast is obvious. They have different kind of hair styles that only work with their long, thick hair and they have naturally rosy cheeks so wear less make-up, not like my eyeliner that can look too hard.

What's she know? I'm glad I'm seeing Marty tonight. He'll make it right.

2ND OCTOBER 1986

Not written for a while because things have just got shittier. Marty came over on Wednesday and finished with me. He just wants to do his own thing, not commit. Basically, do something not with me. Be with someone, anyone, other than me. He said he'd smile if he saw me happy with someone else. Can you believe that? I mean, what do you do with that? I flippin' love him and he's saying that crap. Like I mean nothing to him. Nothing at all.

I didn't let on to him that I was all that bothered, of course. Made it pretty easy for him to do it and get out of here. But I've been a mess for a few days. I just wanted to sleep through it. Get a few days to clear my head. I didn't think anyone would notice, but Debbie did come in my room, after not seeing me for a day, and got concerned over the Temazepam bottle on my floor. It wasn't full and they were quite out of date anyway. I just wanted to sleep.

5TH OCTOBER 1986

5TH OCTOBER 1986

Well, that was a bummer! Talk about embarrassing. There we were, all visiting our second placement wards and flippin' Sharpe (had to be) insists we take our cardies off when we're leaving the school. Well, there am I, looking like I've been in a cat fight with red scratches up my arms. Stupidly superficial. Well, that might not be a bad thing 'cause I suppose deep cuts would have given the game away. But, of course, some people noticed and joked about me being a right mess; 'What have you been doing?'

I just shrugged it off and gave some very lame excuse about getting something out of a bush and getting all these scratches. Debbie caught my eye and we connected in a brief smile. I'm glad she's here. She said something to me the other day about using a razor, but I was in and out of sleep, so I'm not sure if she was talking about herself or not.

. . .

Just back from seeing Lorraine. I missed last week's session. Just couldn't do it. She didn't seem to care. I don't think she missed me.

She was on about some abstract bubble thing, but I've got to admit it's got me thinking. She was saying how babies get born into this automatic bubble, that just exists without question and gets filled, if they're lucky, with love and acceptance and all the good things we need to be healthy. It's made of something impermeable that completely surrounds it, with no way of getting in or out unless, in really sad cases, it erupts. But she said that rarely happens and only when it didn't get filled with adequate good stuff. She said the colour of this invisible bubble, if you try to visualise it, is oranges and yellows, like a warming fire. It glows when energised because everything contained in it is understood and in balance. It contains the baby and the person nurturing it and you have a different bubble for each special person in your life, I guess. So, like, I definitely have one for Sonia and one for my baby brother.

So, when you leave your natural parent, you take that bubble with you, but it can't really be filled by that person anymore. It might contain enough heat to keep it powerful, but it might be empty. But it won't go. It can't not be part of you. And the adoptive parent can't enter it and fill it for you; they have to create a bubble of their own and fill it with everything from scratch. They mustn't ignore your previous bubbles, but they are yours alone. Theirs can't be made of the same natural substance, so they hopefully create something as similar as possible and pull it tightly shut with a drawstring. It can't be complete with no seal like the natural one. It's always going to have a weak spot where it's closed together.

Lorraine reckons I somehow seeped through the draw-string of the one my mum made. My adoptive mum. So, I'm floating in the atmosphere…lost as an astronaut away from the moon's surface, without communication with Earth. Without gravity. No, she didn't say that bit about being in space. That's me imagining what she means. Because that's how I feel when I'm so alone, and scared, and lost.

I asked her why my mum would have let me slip out. Why she didn't pull it tighter. But I didn't need her answer 'cause I know how it was. She'd had enough of me; I'd pushed her too far. She was the one encouraging me to get more 'O' Level's when I only got two at school. After a year at FE college, she was on my back to go into nursing; practically filled the application form in. I thought hair-dressing would be good and was chuffed to get my job sweeping up hair and making tea. Just as a way in. But she was having none of that, 'Not my girl.'

'Well, I'm not. Am I.'

I wish I hadn't said that to her.

15TH Oct 1986

Oh Diary! Delicious name to add to your pages…Andy. Andy. Andy. So, Debbie hung out with a lot of guys at her old school and the other night, a couple of new ones came over. They are mates of one of her friends, so she doesn't know Andy well herself, but she kind of knows everyone a little from home, 'cause it's not a big place and her parent's have always lived there.

Well, this Andy stands out from the others 'cause he's not a weed-head and is really into keeping fit and plays a lot of rugby. He's intelligent as, and I feel right out of my depth, but God! He's gorgeous. Suppose opposites attract 'cause he's into me. Like big time. We can't get enough of each other. I just want to be with him every moment now. He feels SO good!! Don't expect much attention, Diary, someone else has got me now!

28TH OCT 1986

Got myself a cat from the rescue place up the road. Just bundled it to me, no questions asked. We're not supposed to have animals in here so I hope it will settle down soon. It's manic at the moment; I came in to find my room a right mess. Everything scattered on the floor and my plant had all the soil chucked out. Think the loon had been running circles round the walls. Maybe it's a witches cat, sensing halloween an' all, cause it's black as a starless night and has a mean scowl. Think Loon would be a better name that Daffodil. Might change that.

31ST OCT 1986

Going to be short entry cause going out for Halloween. There's a party on downstairs but we'll probably end up going to The Wellington, like usual. I'm just waiting for Andy. He's going to use my face paint once he gets here so I hope he's not running late. Still totally in love…so that's what I've been up to!

Started the new placement and it's going really well. I don't see a lot of the ward sister cause she carries the medical bleep a lot of the time, but she's really nice. You can tell her staff think a lot of her and they are really happy and relaxed. They're allowed to do fun things, like one of them, Bridget, sings while she does the morning drug round. Just silly, daft songs but she makes everyone smile and it's a great start to the day. She seems to really like me. I don't know why. But I kind of feel I can be myself with them.

One half of the ward is Neurology and the other is Dermatology. It's split between two consultants so kind of feels like two different wards but that makes it really interesting, and you can't really get bored. The patients vary in age and some of their cases are really sad. There's a lady in there with MS and she just hasn't got anywhere else to live. She's bed-bound and needs loads of help. She couldn't manage without full-time carers. Her husband comes in to see her every day, but he's with someone else now, and she knows about that. Isn't that sad?

I like dressing the leg ulcers best. Well, they stink something bad, I mean REALLY bad, an odour all of their own. The sticky disturbed layers removed with sterile wipes, plentiful in their hues of human decay, but it's good work. You get them cleaned up and looking smart again and have time for a right old chat while you're doing it. But there's this lady in a side room whose bedsores I hate doing. She's like a beached whale…really, she is. I don't mean to be cruel, but she's huge; she'd spill over the edge if it wasn't for the cot sides. I've never seen anyone so large. So, she can't move, and we can't really do much to change her position and her skin's all breaking down. While she's alive. Well, she kind of is. Her mind's left, I think. She won't chat. She doesn't speak at all really, maybe an occasional grunt or sigh.

Her husband comes in every day, too. He tries to get her to drink the liquid food, help her with the straw 'cause there's no way she can sit up. I've been trying to encourage her to take some too, but she's having none of it. I talk to her about how things got this way, how she can try and turn it back, but she's got no fight. She's given up. Left the room. How can someone be THAT humongous and yet not eat a thing?

He's here!!! Lisa's Lover! Cheerio.

3rd Nov 1986

Loon couldn't stay. She couldn't be a house cat anymore than a buffalo could have come for tea in my room. I feel bad about it, but we just didn't connect. I'm thinking I could turn my bed over and create a space for a rabbit in the corner of the room. I like sleeping on just a mattress anyway, and the nasty vinyl flooring lends itself to being a litter tray.

Thought I'd catch you up with a change I've decided to make. I'm not going to visit Lorraine anymore. I just don't need it. She like digs and wants me to look inside every-thing too much, always asking for too many feelings and then kind of dumping them on me when the hour's up. She can move on, but I'm left with stuff I didn't want to get out in the first place.

Yesterday, she was on about Sonia again, 'What if', 'Do you ever', 'How about…' How about you shut the fuck up, that's what I want to say!! I put all that away years ago and don't have any interest in finding her. She'd be looking for me if she wanted to get back together. I'm not going to go knocking on someone's door who doesn't know me and probably doesn't want to. Like I could ever find out where she is now, anyway? She's an adult. Free of their bloody system. They haven't got tabs on us anymore. I've had enough of them having a hold on me. Knowing what I think. Well, thinking they do. Stuff it. I'll be fine now, 'cause I've got Andy and the staff at work really like me, too. I just wish I could stay there permanently and not have to move onto the next placement in five weeks' time.

5 TH Nov 1986

I got to go down to Dermatology clinic today. Just for the experience. Bloody boring, like proper mind-numbing standing around waiting on doctors, until this girl comes in and like throws the atmosphere on its head. It was like everyone sat up, slapped themselves awake and switched on their empathy buttons.

She was called Julie and the staff all seem to know her 'cause she must have been in and out since her accident. When she was ten, a firework exploded in her face, so you can maybe guess what her face looks like. Well, maybe not. A lot of it melted. Her sight was saved in one eye which is, they tell me, amazing.

She's had lots of ops with plastics, and they've done as best they could, but she doesn't look like anyone I've ever seen before. Her skin is tight and shiny in places and looks pulled too taunt as she speaks. They told me not to mention her family because it's a sad story and she doesn't see any of them. Well, that did it for me; you can imagine how that struck a chord. My heart was on my sleeve for her, especially when we started talking.

We were alone in the room, waiting for Dr Walsh to come through. I had been a lot more able with the staff nurse being in there too, but she'd got called to help someone out in the waiting room and left me there stranded. Idle chit-chat seemed inadequate and the fact we were close in age made it even harder to say anything without it seeming like sympathetic mush.

'How long ago was your accident?' Lame attempt scores zero, I remember tutting internally.

'Seven years ago, today.' She couldn't really smile but her eye's sparkle disclosed a bright soul, and the tone of her voice was light enough. She seemed amused by the achievement of challenging her likely time on earth, rather than suffocating in self pity. There was wet around her eye and she kept having to dab at it. Not tears of sorrow, but an overproduction and disturbance of nature's delicate linings; a constant reminder.

'Oh yeah. It's firework night,' I bit my lip at my planned careless continuation of this line. Instead, I asked her if she was still at school.

'No. I've kind of been home-schooled but stopped that last year.'

'Do you still have to do exams when you're learning that way?' My mind had jumped from school uniformed images of jeering, mean faces, pushing up too close, to an isolated lone figure in a room too vast to nurture her loss.

'Well, if you want. It's really kind of flexible. I'd quite like to be a nurse, give a bit back. They've always been so kind to me.' As she wiped her eye once more, I noticed her hand's skin was like smooth, white china contrasting sharply with the angry carmine tones of her face's altered flesh.

'You could do that. Get a few 'O' Levels and off you'd go. I scraped myself in!'

'How many do you need?'

'Five. One's supposed to be Human Biology, but I completely flunked science. I don't really know how I did get in! The lady who interviewed me must have been kind,' I told her honestly and without embarrassment. I learnt to accept my place and limited expectation long ago.

'She must have looked past that then. Seen something in you.'

And that was it. One of those rare and truly beautiful moments. A look shared; a knowledge passed; a connection. Like she'd spotted Lisa and held out her hand. A warmth to cherish and recall when needing to stoke the ashes after the hope of heat is gone.

We were interrupted by the consultant coming in, followed briskly by his entourage of student, registrar, and nurse. And that was it, exchange over. Shift nearly spent. But Julie's stayed with me. Sharp edges jarring my conscience like the blade I cut myself with later that evening. But there's no relief. The pain's more intense. What is it that's causing the build-up of pressure in my head? Why do I want to know this stranger more? Feel we could somehow connect. Help each other heal? Why did I find it hard to walk out the room, knowing I'd never see her again?

22ND DEC 1986

Good job you can't talk, Diary of mine. You give too much away just with all your torn out pages between my entries. The words removed that were scratchy and harsh, or with pen too flimsily held in a semi-conscious hand. The words that didn't know how to form even when written and the empty gaps that contain more than any writing ever could.

Christmas is always hard, but I don't know why. I listen to Joni Mitchell and sink into a place of comfort but the nearer it gets to the twenty-fifth, the harder it is to wrap the dream around me; to feel cushioned on my sides by the dark, safe place of sleep.

'It's coming on Christmas…'

27ᵀᴴ Dec 1986

Well, that went as well as expected. Two days at home too much. What is it about being home, when we're all there and things are supposed to be fun and loving and, I don't know…easy? How come I always feel on the outside looking in. Can't put my words right or never get taken how I'm meaning. Always ruin everything; turn milk sour.

I know I'm not a bad person. How can they always twist my words, so it sounds like something mean? Troublesome. How do they always make me feel so inadequate and small? So invisible?

I'm starting on Children's Ward in two days' time and when I looked round it was bloody awful. All these children crying and parents demanding, and nurses snapping and being as starched as their stupid white caps. I don't think I want to do this job anymore. It's not me. I think I'll find something else. Carrot packing was better. Maybe I'll call Lorraine. At least she tolerated me for an hour a week.

I wish Andy hadn't left me.

I'm going out to buy a rabbit.

TEA WITH JULIE

*J*ulie Marr's family were infamous in the Fens. All the men had been, or would be, in prison, so Julie's dad currently resided there. They were thieves and the Marr's bloodline was as part of the fen as the dykes that ran through them. They were its bleak winter fields and the smell of summer in the steaming rain from hot, tarmac roads; strawberries at best and carrots at worst; the autumn piles of the sugar beet harvest, the promise and scar of the agricultural fields.

Her house was squashed into a mean terrace, with no front gardens or features. The brick simple and anonymous, telling no history other than the engraved '1913' on the middle house. The year after the Titanic sunk; the year before the Great War began. What talk must have slipped into the mortar. What grief and trouble must have been rubbed into the sand.

Erected on the road that led nowhere and opposite the great span of the dark River Nene, the row looked like a 'lift the flap' on an otherwise barren page. The silt of the river, high on each side of the liquid mud, hid many secrets. It was the perfect place for throwing things in a hurry. All her relatives must have lived by the river; to reluctantly gift it valuable hoards when the law came but also to chuck in what they saw as rubbish. Julie's Alsatian had delivered puppies and one was allowed to stay. The rest were given to the river.

We played outside, in her small backyard, with the chained mother and her itchy, warm, milk-bellied pup. The bare kennel, an empty tea chest, was chewed and disowned, replaced with a deep, muddy hole dug beneath it. I remember the empty tin bowl, which clattered as the chain hit against it. The smell of their waste lay heavy in the moist November air. No comfort. On reflection, I can see that comfort would invite softness and that had no place here.

I was interested in the terraced yards; how they were so close and different to my garden with flowers and a pond, at home. I was inspired by them and made paper people and similar scenes, which I could then stand up and put tight against each other. I played with these set-ups for long Sundays, and they brightened the darkness and wet of monotonous, winter days.

Inside Julie's kitchen, her mum had the radio on, and it felt cheery. Rod Stewart was singing 'Da Ya Think I'm Sexy?' and Julie's mum was enjoying it. She was singing along, whilst making us tea. The toast smelt good. I liked that just Julie and I sat at the table for our beans on toast. It was informal and I appreciated it, in contrast to our mannered meals at home. I'd never had beans on toast as a main meal before.

Upstairs, Julie had a room next to her brother Paul's. He was a year younger and must have been playing out. You had to walk through Julie's room to reach his, which was like a small after-thought stuck to the end of the house. I remember being in awe of his boxing bag. It seemed enormous, filling the small space but so cool. There was a leathery smell to it, mingled with that of bed-wetted sheets.

Julie walked me home, down her road and into the lane where I lived at the far end. The half-light had come, and the promised rain started to drizzle. As we passed the big houses on the corner, I looked down the Gothic vicarage drive. Its fallen mulberry tree twists looking malignant in the haze; as if turning into jealous spirits which would follow behind us, dragging the dark closer and waiting for our cries. This would revive the ghosts and they would then be able to soar above us like burning embers rising from their devil's fire.

The three, short figures walking towards us, in shadow from their dark clothes and the drab grey, broke my imaginings and returned me to the dank early evening. They looked chirpy and flippant as they brought their ciggies to their lips, held in thumb and forefinger, and then returned to cupped hands, mimicking adult behaviour, and preventing the rain from dampening the cigarettes glow. Purposefully striding mid-lane, the three looked to pass us by without acknowledgment. It was Julie who called out to her brother, seeing the sack of straw he was dragging,

'What you doin'?'

He continued without answer but one of their cousins dug him in the ribs, 'We'll need her, to knock on the doors. Can't see us three gettin' much.'

'Yeh,' nodded Paul. Turning to his sister only, he grunted they were making a Guy. Would be making some money. She could come. But not get as much as them.

'See ya tomorrow,' she brightly threw back at me. I, aware of my place and knowing our time was at an end (regardless of whether or not I too was invited), smiled and nodded, turning for the last of my short walk home.

I envied her freedom. I imagined her playing out for endless hours. Able to feel adult and not confined by her ten-year-old self. The dark bringing no curfew or restraint to the making of their Guy. With Guy Fawke's Night tomorrow, I knew the straw would be stuffed in old clothes tonight, the face drawn on and the creation wheeled about proudly after school tomorrow, hopeful of cash.

'Does it look good?' I asked Julie once we got a chance to talk at break the next day at school.

'What?'

'Your Guy. Did you make it look good?'

For a moment there was something unreadable in Julie's eyes. She kicked at the pile of collected wet leaves close by. Held in damp weight they gave none of the exciting crunch. No twirling autumnal colours were released to the air.

'We left it. Paul nicked some of mum's tights and she saw. Making Guys is for babies anyway.' Her voice gave her care away. Although sounding hard, I sensed the disappointment and hurt that it covered. They must have got in trouble.

'Shall we collect some bottles on the way home? I'll walk your way if you like.' My offer felt lame, but I wanted away from the weight of the moment. I wanted to breathe fresher air, but the morning's fog had left its heavy particles in the atmosphere, and I still smelled its moisture. It seemed to cling on to me. It plastered my straight mousy hair to my head, and it felt oppressive.

'There might be some chucked in the field,' she supposed. 'We could look about. I can't be long though…Paul might get some fireworks off our uncle. I'll want to see them go off.' Her voice was singing with laughter in its notes. The thought of finding some bottles to take back to the corner shop in exchange for some penny sweets had worked its ten-year-old magic. Hope was back with us, to fill another dreary school day.

I went to Smedleys with my family. They did a firework display every year on their factory's land, opposite the school. The bonfire blazed with a heat too intense to face. Its contents cracked and hissed and the smoky smell was as sharp as the scented steam rising from the cupped tomato soup in my hands. The bite of the cold air on my cheek furthest from the fire, while the other felt ready to melt. Like I was halved; two different people, like Siamese twins. I wondered which felt better, who to go with.

I didn't think of Julie. Of what her fireworks looked like. Whether Paul had got any. I guessed it would be bad news if any pets strayed their way or a child happened to cross their paths whilst the lads' pockets itched with such lethal weapons. I didn't think it would be Julie.

The tale seemed round the school before the gate was opened next morning. All the kids down Julie's road had come out to see why the ambulance was there. Blue light spinning in the still, black air. Everything suspended. Moments hung on overhead branches, dipping with the weight.

'All I remember is her mum crying. She didn't stop. She wouldn't talk to them. They kept asking her 'What's her name? What's her name, Love?' and Paul yelling like he was mad, like no one could hear him, 'It was a bloody accident. An accident.'

My friend, Sarah, clasped her hands, swayed a little, telling me what she'd witnessed. Eager to be the source of news but wishing it wasn't so. I stuck my nose under my scarf, watched her breath puff into the air and remain, unmoving. As if her sentences weren't acceptable and wouldn't pass on to the great kingdom of words.

Julie had been handed a tin. 'Just hold it, while we light 'em over 'ere', her cousin had said. She hadn't thought anything of it. Nor had they. The lit firework inside would burst out and make her jump the most she ever had. No threat of mum could compare to the shock her gut was about to get. The lads smirked and clapped each other's backs.

'Hey, keep it away from your face! Point it that way,' Paul had shouted, turning back to look at her waiting obediently some metres away from them.

·⁂·

I'M HERE NOW, forty years on, standing by the river. I daren't ask around for her because what would I say? She wouldn't want my pity. I don't know where they went once she got out of hospital. The memories are over me and crushing with their weight; they push me to the ground. It's wet and the tired grass is hidden under fallen leaves and compact dandelions, that somehow survive all. I let myself cry. It's been too long kept in. The guilt for being born luckier; the pain of not saving her from it; the pointless imagining of what her life could have been and how painful and hard it must be now, how tough it was anyway; the loss of a friend.

Nothing seems so changed around here. The terrace still holds secrets behind its walls. The river still flows its sludgy straight path, letting some things stay and become part of it, while allowing others to pass through to glimpse the wide-open sea.

THINGS UNKNOWN

*T*heir intense, passionate relationship meant that sharing any finer details of each other's lives had been lost in the whirlwind. Clare was as surprised at the Volkswagen camper that drove into her life on the morning of travel, as she had been when her brown haired, wiry strip of a man had proposed to her a week after meeting.

The chug of the diesel engine was loud, and its rumble had stirred the quiet of her Sunday morning newspaper street. She had felt the prickle of neighbours twitched net curtains on the back of her neck, as she stroked the yellow side of the aged van.

'This yours?' she asked with astonishment. Where had he been keeping it? They'd been with each other every day since meeting a month ago with no mention of this little beauty.

'Said I'd get us there, didn't I?' Shaun's reply didn't give much away and reflected his bright and often flippant nature. He rubbed his hands in childlike glee and raised his chin to acknowledge the good weather, 'This is going to be fun!'

Leaving her rented room in the Edwardian house-share, felt almost as defiant as remarkable. As if her time had come, her number was at last called, her life could begin at twenty-three. The repetitive days at her uninspiring job, the well-worn walk home, the boring rituals of hanging wet clothes dangerously on her inadequate storage heaters and the unwholesome, lonely TV meals could be waved goodbye.

Giving the turn-of-the-century house a farewell glance, she smiled to herself, realising that this here, this exact moment, year 2015, was a monumental turn in her own life. She felt as if everyone should be out on the street clapping, throwing roses at her feet. In her mind, a thousand cheers let their good wishes fly to the sky, to float above them on the clouds of cotton wool.

Chatting over and singing to their limited classic tapes of Bob Marley and Fleetwood Mac, her mood had matched Shaun's lightheartedness. They were on an adventure; had ripped their boxes open. Relieved that the tape could work in the questionable player, she let the songs flow one to the other, without interference. Always one to play favourites over and over, skipping all the in-between, her fingers had itched to punch the forward wind, but the buttons looked severe in their warning that they would pop off and remain in the footwell for the rest of the journey if approached.

Even the endlessly flat, open fields, with their expressionless, straight rivers of mud didn't dampen her spirits, as they chugged towards the Lincolnshire border to pass through and eventually leave the fenlands behind. Stopping for petrol and a bacon butty two hours in, Clare marvelled at the familiar and yet strange scenery they stood in,

'My dad's from round here. Originally. You know, like, they've always been Fen folk on his side. I used to think I must have been adopted, come from someone else's genes, 'cause all I can see is sugar beet and carrots. I can't appreciate the place. It's not in my bones.' The fields around them were busy with pickers and the lorries slowly loaded high with the produce. The flapping covers now removed to expose green mound after mound of cabbages.

'Where do you see your bones belonging, then?' Shaun's voice had seemed a little mocking, as he'd chanced a sip and blown the froth off his steaming coffee, 'This not good enough for ya?'

'No. Not that. Just that I love hills…and the sea. Someplace that those two meet would be pretty special, wouldn't it? I suppose that's what attracted me to our honeymoon spot. When we cross back onto the mainland, we can explore the highlands too.'

'Yeh, but you couldn't have picked a further bloody island, could ya? It's so high it's almost Arctic.'

'Think we'd hit Iceland first, actually!' Clare had studied the map closely in her anticipation of their trip. She had learned the near-by Lewis Island names and been fascinated to discover the size of Greenland and the isolation of Iceland but now, although not intended, her retort had an edge of superiority that looked to poke at Shaun's surprisingly frail ego,

'Got a fucking 'A' level in Geography, did ya?' His growl had stunned Clare for a moment, but the smell of strawberries wafted to her as she passed the open stall window, and she let their sweet scent override his bitter comment.

'Now these, never taste so good as when picked straight from the field, with a light summer rain washed over the promised sun-kissed bite,' she giggled, and popped one in her mouth as if making an advert.

'Like I don't know about strawberry picking! I would have had my chips up to weigh three times while you giggled and ate in the rows,' Shaun's humour restored, as swiftly as a cloud passing the sun, allowed the fruit's treat to bond them once more. The warming rays graced their bodies and the punnet alike, encouraging the couple to devour one after the other, laughing at the juicy mess on their chins and fruits-stain on their fingers. As Shaun laughed, he gave a smidgeon of his life away,

'My grandad's sisters live somewhere really near here but I don't know them. What's that make them to me anyway? They thought they were better than the rest of us, so they were thrown off. It's important to know who you are, my dad always told us.'

'And do you?' Clare's expression looked as if she'd challenge that, knowing so little of Shaun's past. In fact, this was the first she'd heard of his dad. She had thought he must have been an absent parent.

''Course I do.' He jumped back into the camper muttering, 'Don't mean you've gotta like it though.' Clare wasn't sure she'd caught his words correctly but sensed any exploration should wait and not taint their trip with heavy or repressed thoughts. Her mind flitted half-heartedly to her own flesh and blood. Heidi, her step-sister, lived in Nottingham so not far off the road they travelled, but the thought of dropping in on her made Clare silently shudder. If she was sober, she'd be up to her eyes in nappies and matters completely alien and confusing to her younger sibling. Clare wasn't convinced that she herself had a maternal bone in her body and secretly hoped Shaun wouldn't be too fussed either way.

At Newark, the slow, tractor-filled roads were replaced instantly by miles of repetitive and ugly A1. Here, the van's story unfolded, and it became clear to Clare that she wasn't the only love in Shaun's life. Superficially, his vehicle wore its age well, with its cushions and paint hiding most of the mildew and rust. Clare could only see their own little dream on wheels.

'Didn't think you were the type for flowery throws!' she chuckled.

'Well, you got me right then. That's my mate's wife, Shirl. They've been lookin' after it for me. Thrilled it all up! Been takin' liberties.'

'I like it. You remember playing Mummies and Daddies at school? It will be like that! Our own little playhouse.'

Shaun had tapped his fingers on his seat. She liked watching him drive. It was like a smooth, choreographed dance; left hand taking the wheel, as he took a deep inhale of his ciggy, and then, swopping driving hands fluidly, his left hand fingers drummed the cushion between his legs, rhythmically and tenderly as if lost in a dream.

'You always do that.' Indicating his habit, she had swung him a cheeky smile, 'Play the drums, did you? Or was it piano lessons?'

Shaun's look had been no more pleasant than cheeky. More a sneer; like bewilderment at her naivety, 'You'll be thinking I was in the bloody choir next.'

'You weren't? I thought I saw you on Songs of Praise when I was younger. Yeh, that's what I thought, when you walked in the pub that Friday night!'

'Ain't you in a cheeky mood, Girl. Bit excited for our trip, are we?' Shaun's smile was rare, but well worth the wait.

Clare grabbed it and sat openly smirking, feeling on top of the world.

'Hey, talking of Songs of Praise, ain't that the Angel of the North?'

'Can't see nothing, Shaun. Where you looking?'

The steel structure was dramatic against the darkening sky and hidden periodically from view,

'There, through the trees on my side. Quite sumthin,' init?' Shaun acknowledged.

'Do you think she's blessing us!'

'Sure! She's like saying, 'Go on Shaun, get along before the storm breaks. Turn off a bit further on, for the road to Gretna Green!'

'Well, it was like we were being looked after getting that cancelled wedding slot, weren't it? I mean, how lucky was that!'

***

THEY STOPPED at their pre-arranged wedding venue for no more than an hour. They had hoped to look round the shops, get a cup of tea, but the increasingly heavy sky had changed to the steel it had been threatening for the last half hour and broke dramatically with arrowlike rain.

To claps of thunder, they repeated their promises whilst standing at the anvil that signified the forging of their bond. The supplied witness also took some photos for them, using Shaun's iPhone.

'Can't see the point in spending money on professional ones when this is so good, but I will get you a better ring soon. Once I get sorted. But there we are…we done it! I'm gonna get ya a band thick enough to put our date on it. On the inside.' Shaun kissed her again, full on, with a force that made her wish they had a hotel room to run to.

'I like that we're married on the seventh of the seventh 2015,' beamed Clare, whose smile shone brighter than any flashy ring could have done, 'My mum had a thing for numbers being neat like that. She'd say it was lucky. Like when my baby brother was born too early. She said he'd make it if he could come that day…the tenth of the tenth 2000.'

'And did he?'

The conversation halted for a moment whilst they jumped back in the van, shielding from the downpour as best they could in their flimsy summer clothes,

'Well. Yeh. He was born that day and his eyes were bright and his cry was loud. He lived for five days so that was something, wasn't it?'

'Depends how ya look at it, I suppose.'

'God no. That was amazing. No one would have predicted he could have made it that far. He had so much stacked against him. But he was a fighter. And we got to know him.'

Shaun considered this whilst twisting his cigarette between finger and thumb. His eyes were awfully sad when he raised them again to Clare, and his words so sorrowful that Clare didn't register the reference to having their own children so much as sensed his pain,

'Let's not make our kids' fighters. I don't want to make my sons beat each other up. I won't kick 'em to make them do it and watch them scrap like it's a game.'

'God no, Shaun! No, I meant he was a strong character. Resilient. Not fighting like that. Is that how it was for you then?'

The shake of his head seemed to toss painful memories more than deny it was so. Again, Clare felt they should come back to this another time. Today mustn't be saddened. Today needed to be the best day,

'My nan told me 'Happy the bride the sun shines on'…she didn't say what happens to the one wed in pissin' rain!' she laughed, determined to let nothing darken this memory.

Shaun grabbed her to him unexpectedly, hungrily, as they dripped on the front seats, shaking themselves like dogs and shuddering from the cold the wet had brought.

❦

THE LENGTH of their journey through Scotland to the arranged remote Scottish island slowly gathered a tension to it as it progressed, as if the storm had attached to them and refused to let go, despite having passed. As if every few miles a new clod of mud stuck to the tyres as they turned, pulling like a weight on the van. It seemed that the sun's disappearance was enough to rob Shaun of any gathered warmth or optimism. Driving past Lockerbie did nothing to lighten the mood. As the unspoken angst gathered, the repetitive scrape of the windowscreen wipers set even Clare's nerves on edge,

'They squeak like hell. New blades would fix it, wouldn't it?'

Shaun's tapping increased in speed.

'Doesn't it get to you?'

Shaun began to hum.

'For God's sakes! That doesn't help.'

'What the hell do you want me to do about it? Right now.
Right here.' His voice was as harsh as loud. Clare instinctively sat straighter, taking her legs down from the glove
compartment ledge. Sharpened and listening for something that she was beginning to feel she had missed; she
was left baffled by her own intuition. Her mumbled 'Ouch'
was timid and quiet but offered with genuine good
humour, as was her learned policy of distraction in times
of encroaching fear or confusion,

'Let's play a game. Did you used to play I Spy an' all that?
Going to my gran's was always a long trip. She was down
in Cornwall. That was my mum's mum...'

'Can you give it a break? I need to concentrate in this
bloody weather. My lights aren't all that either.' He winced,
as if in physical pain.

'Hey, don't take it personally. She's an old girl. I like her.
She can rest plenty when we get there. Watch us making
love, drinking in the sunset, swimming to the nearby island.
It's only a mile away...can you swim that far?'

'Why would I want to swim? I'm not a fuckin' eel, am I?'

'Alright. Only asking! Didn't you get taught at school?'

'We didn't live in water. Why would I need to flippin'
swim?'

His tapping had become purposeful with a steady, heavy
thud.

'Hey, Shaun. I'll teach you. Didn't you go with your family
to the local swimming pool? Even Wisbech must have had

one? Fun once you were in. But, God! Always freezin' in the changing rooms and you could never get properly dry. Your knickers wouldn't get past your knees; socks stuck on your heel...'

Clare stopped, noticing Shaun's tapping had become more of a thump. Stretching her hand gently to his, he swiped it away roughly, 'Why couldn't you have booked somewhere nearer? There's no hills anymore anyway. It's as boring and flat here as it is at home.' His eyes had blazed and yet been cold.

'We must still be in the lowlands. It will change, you'll see. The highlands are mountainous, aren't they? Ben Nevis an' all that. Full of glens and crags.'

Clare was grateful when Shaun turned off the M74 and found a track that seemed far enough from the road to be unnoticed. She thought the nearest signed place, East Kilbride, was probably not the most welcoming title for your honeymoon night. She laughed it off though, as they settled to recover from the day's long drive. As they pulled the settee apart and made the bed, routing in boxes for glasses and pouring their wine, some colour came back to Shaun's demeanour and he lost his exasperated expression,

'We must be well over halfway by now, hey Clare?' but hope was definitely clearer than fact in his newfound optimism. With his jaw muscles softened and playfulness restored, he felt as solid and reliable as before when he pushed Clare down to their wedding bed.

She woke at dawn, with bright light streaming through the thin van curtains. She studied the resting face of her still-sleeping man and lightly twiddled his hair, scruffily boy-like and cheeky rather than ungroomed. It was gently bleached by the recent good weather, and he looked ravishing to his keen bride. His skin had tanned in the last two weeks and Clare gently stroked the almost invisible blond hairs over his forearm tattoo. Only his reluctance to stir showed that he had not rested enough but, when he eventually opened his eyes, they looked more tired than the evening before.

Clare wiped the window's condensation and peered through her circle. The unknown area, with weathered crofts softened and dreamlike in the light of the dawn, refreshed her spirits and restored her hope of the promise of change. She breathed it in and held her breathe whilst she sorted it into her mind's compartments, willing the memories to stay sharp and clear and not escape her. She'd never left England before. She wanted to ask Shaun if he had but sensed it was best to observe the quiet. He still seemed reluctant to wake and she supposed it was with the thought of all the travelling yet to do. Maybe she should have chosen somewhere closer. She wished she had passed her driving test after so many attempts. Then, at least they could share the driving and she'd feel less guilty about her romantic, but perhaps unwise, decision.

Returning to the journey after breakfast, Clare had dozed a fair bit and at last stretched her arms and back to see it was past midday. Even by early afternoon, the tedium of the drive and the line of the road limited the joy to be found in window gazing. The tape recorder had died last night, chewing her favourites into a tangle, resemblant of a matted dreadlock. Shaun had now, at last, picked up a radio station he could tolerate, and his irritation had turned more to a whinge. The van smelt musty and damp, its swinging apple air freshener not quite as sweet as yesterday but instead rather nauseating, mixed with the lingering odour of their greasy chip supper.

'Wake up, Girl. It's ferry time,' he had said with intrepid relief, seeing before them a distant land seemingly unreachable over the north Atlantic's charging waves and mysterious depths. Shadowed distantly behind such choppy and demanding water, the island looked lost and forgotten rather than inviting. The bumps and jolts to get the trembling vehicle over the ramp and ropes of the ferry felt risky, but, thankfully, it didn't take too long for the island to be reached. The engine's diesel hum agreed to restart and both Shaun and Clare's anxiety was replaced with smiles of relief.

'I couldn't resist the description on Airbnb; quaint, idyllic and remote. The kind of place for lovers!' she laughed, rubbing his rough hand in hers. 'I added that last bit!' she giggled, to no response. Shaun scanned the island with different eyes to her own.

·:Ⅲ·

AFTER TWO DAYS OF LONG, sticky travel the sight that beheld them was astonishing only in its devastation. The 'quaint' was a ruin, the 'idyllic' a hell and the 'remote' led Shaun to instant despair.

'What the …', he screamed, pulling at his unkept hair, 'you havin' a laugh?' He had glared at his equally puzzled newlywed.

'Oh my God! It's been mis-sold!' But Clare's voice held a hint of wonder, as she picked her way through the old croft door, hanging on its long-rusted hinges and refusing to widen. She sucked at her finger, where a splinter had lodged its sharp point,

'Look here, Shaun…there's birds nesting in here. Be quiet when you come.'

'That's the only bloody thing that will nest in there. For God's sake, look at the roof! You can't call that blown straw a thatch. Must be full of rats and spiders. We'll have to go back to the mainland. We've wasted our precious money.' His words were spat with fury.

'There's only one ferry a day, Shaun. We'll have to kip here tonight. Don't see it as a waste though...your van has a bed and we've got our supplies, haven't we?' Her rhetorical question was met with a soulful wail from her man.

'It feels like I'll be punished forever!' he suddenly cried, falling to his knees. His clouded face showed hints of boy-like drama but there was something in his tone that seemed too dark for that of a child. Tearing at the purple heather around him and seeing nothing in his now hateful eyes but dried grass, he brought his hand furiously to his flowing tears. To Clare there was a hush. A moment of odd still-ness and pause. The wind seemed to have stopped, as if waiting for more explanation. The temperature seemed to have dropped to a chill beyond snow.

'What are you talking about?' Clare's voice revealed some of the nauseating panic that she sensed arising. Closing her eyes, she wished this scene away; to be taken by the rhythmic crash of the nearby waves; to realise it was only the effect of a troublesome journey and, although inappro-priate, was nothing more. But, on opening her eyes, nothing had altered; Shaun was still sitting back on his heels, looking lost to the ground he'd fallen to. He looked as if he was protracting, disappearing down a tunnel, becoming so small that maybe she could lift him in her hands and nurture this anger away. Bring him back with a kiss.

The venom in his words shoved dreamy images away and she was again instantly aware of his full-sized presence,

'I've done time. Quite a lot of time. Haven't been out two months and this bloody happens.' Noticing the confusion and horror mixed in her eyes, he glared a reply, 'I would have told ya. I just wanted to start again, didn't I? Is that so wrong?' His voice was raised and mean. It sounded detached. No longer belonging to the man she had shared the last four weeks with.

'What were you in for? Why didn't you let me know?' Clare could hardly recognise her own flabbergasted voice. It was trying to escape, to run with her questions. Could a gull swoop to her, carry her from this reality? An eagle? She'd heard of sea eagles, and here, in this unknown mystical place, they could be giants. All she could centre on was visualising the span of their wings as she swayed on the spot. What was firm, rocky heather terrain had turned in an instant to quicksand.

'Manslaughter,' he stated. 'I bottled this guy, and it did more than I'd meant. It's my temper. I get too angry.'

His eyes held nothing she had seen before. They seemed to hold nothing.

'Did you know him? Like, was he a friend?'

'I wouldn't bottle a mate! He was looking for a fight. Winding me up. I know what you're thinking…would I hurt you?' The battle in his eyes gave way to his original character, a gentle pain swept through them replacing his cavalier harshness. Although reassuring, it could no longer tempt Clare to step towards him.

'Well, yeh. There is that. I'm not going to lie. I haven't known anything about you it seems.'

'Have I hidden my temper? Haven't you seen how quick I fly? You can't blame me, if you only saw what you wanted to see, Clare.'

The gulls swooped in and out of the ruin, their beating wings muffled in the thoughts processing in her head. She looked to the thin gold band on her ring finger. Wed. To a stranger. Turning it round and round, her eyes stayed down considering her options. Did it change what he meant to her? Would her heart beat less frantically when their eyes locked? When she held his body? Thought of him being hers? She knew she still wanted him. God, she was head-over-heels for him. Could she help him? She wasn't looking for an easy life. She'd been bored for so long. Never expecting anyone to want her. To be hers. She wasn't going to throw it all away now, was she? She fell on her knees to take his hands in hers, to look at his eyes and read their truth,

'Will you talk to me? Tell me where you think your anger comes from? Will you trust me? I don't want to live like Bonnie and Clyde, but I'm OK with this, if it's in the past.'

Behind Shaun, the sea splashed against the rocky island edge, filling the fauna-rich rock pools and seeming to listen with intrigue. What would this Fen Tiger do?

'I was born angry. My dad was angry and his, too: his before that no doubt. Always in and out the nick. Always feeling bad about themselves. It's not something you can fix, really. It's in my blood.'

'I see more in you than that though, don't I,' Clare's realisation processing as she spoke, 'In some ways it's good I didn't know you were just out of prison, or I would have made assumptions.'

'They would have been right.'

'I would have missed all the other stuff, though. How funny you are, how kind. How you try really hard to make things good. How careful you are to be there on time. And you're the world's best cuddler!'

His shy laugh encouraged her closer. They sat side by side, leaning on each other, oblivious to their wet bottoms on the still-soaked grass. They watched the sky. The clouds were thin lines spreading through the horizon, promising of a break in the rain. The sea seemed to quieten, hold its breath. Can he keep this one? Can she manage him?

'Why did your dad go to prison?'

'Oh! He was in and out all the time. Nicking stuff mostly. But it started for him when he was really young. He accidently burnt his sister's face off with a firework. Went to Borstal and, what would have been his path anyway, in time, started from that point on. He was the youngest Marrs to get put away.'

'Do you know it was an accident?'

'No doubt about it. He was broken by it. Bloody kids messing about, that's all they were. Once you're in a family like ours, though, you don't really stand a chance. You need something to take you out of it, but I couldn't find nothin'. Not good at much 'cept fighting. Didn't do well at school.'

'Yeh, but like you say, a lot of that is influenced by other people's expectations of you. You're bright as a button. I know that. There's no reason you shouldn't have done OK at school if you were inspired and felt valued.'

Something in him seemed to break a little at her last few words. More tears fell and the sea seemed to clap, releasing a smashing thunder of a wave. They'll be alright, it seemed to know. As long as she can tap into his softer, true side. As long as he learns to swim.

THE LEVERET

*H*eidi was no longer sure of exactly how old
she was. She had stopped counting at around
thirty-two, as her life's path had altered and markers of
days, never mind occasions, had disappeared. She knew
that it was a long time since she'd left them all. With her
husband and baby Frank still sleeping, it was her toddler's
stirring that had snapped her frozen shell into action. She
knew it was now or never, as she had silently closed the
door on her life.

There had been no tears and barely a plan. She just knew,
inherently, she was in the wrong life. Driving some distance
away, the only hint of her route was the train station the
Beetle was parked at. From there, with the daily maximum
allowance of cash withdrawn, she disappeared from their
lives. Her purse, with driving licence and bank cards, her
keys to house and car, simply placed in the glove compartment and abandoned.

Her escape to the sea, some hundred and forty miles away,
at first had felt temporary, as she moved between run-down
hotels every night. Never catching the other shadows who
frequented their rooms only for sleep; with mattresses

always warm from the back-to-back workers, yawning in from a nightshift while others dragged out just after dawn. The oppressive gloom was increased by the recurrent nicotine shading, the faded dry flower displays, the tourist pamphlets untouched on the counters of the minute receptions, squeezed to the back of skinny, dark entrance halls. As if the buildings themselves gave deliberately wicked kicks instead of welcome to their guests' fractured souls, which felt as worthless as the places they stayed in, believing they deserved nothing more.

The shame Heidi felt in failing to be grateful, full of joy, consumed her; making it impossible to disclose to any who might listen what thoughts filled her head. How could she leave so much? What was wrong with her? How could she be so cruel? Guilt and so much more buried her at night, as she tossed and turned, back drenched in sweat, staring wide eyed up at the nasty hotels' yellowed ceilings. Tears were spent. Something numbing took over in the day but at night the prowling, malicious darkness was full of condemnation.

Before her children were born, she had doubted she could mother them; when faced with the reality, all her fears were magnified and given full stage. She could still hear the white-noise machines that she'd bought to help soothe them; so many posts on Facebook parenting groups had said that they'd work. She had watched her babies sleeping on screens that could listen and aid, but this was so constant it had become an addiction; like the detectors for cot death placed under their mattresses.

And then there had been the mothers who wanted their baby a certain weight by Christmas. At first, she had laughed to herself, thinking they were a turkey replacement, but the statistics and percentages, the charts for baby development offered online and the books of techniques, the comparing and competing…My God! She had just wanted them always close, to roll up in their smell, to feel the flutter of their breathing against her own chest; stroking their soft baby down and hearing their little clicks and coos would be the highlight of her day. But it came entombed in a fear, a darkness that pinned her down as if she was held by savage wolves. In her mind, her babies sweet breath was threatened by formidable panting; she couldn't stop the saliva-dripping tongues.

Now, she woke fitfully in the alien rooms, disorientated, and lost; searching for her children, stretching her ears to know where they were, holding her breath to not crowd the noise. Then, twisting her fists into the mattress to strangle the pain, like a foetus, she buried her head deep in her chest, as if searching for the very centre of herself…only to be thwarted, for it would seem there was nothing there. She might hum an old tune mixed up and confused, so that the nursery rhyme was barely detectable, but the repetitive noise would let her breathing calm down.

Heidi had intended on getting work, being independent whilst she tried to find herself; discover what life she could possibly fit, whilst enabling her family to get on better without her. But her mind was unfocused, her hair quickly becoming matted and clothes smelly. Self-care was as lost as her own soul. She plucked at the wool of her cardy, she picked at the mean hotel pillows desperate to find down; in her mind a nest was needed, a safe place to rest.

Cash disappeared in a matter of weeks, leaving the streets as the only shelter for the challenging nights and food to be picked out of bins. Maybe, reversing her sleeping habits would help throw off the demons that chased in her head and swam in her veins? So, she hopefully curled ball-like in bus shelters and fields whilst others around her got on with their day. Like a hare, in the dry; like a fox in the dark. Watching and listening with senses more alert than ever before.

A year or so later, remarkably, someone recognised her from a missing poster, up on a tree three counties from where they'd spotted her whilst holidaying. Using their mobile, they eagerly shared their discovery and within a few hours Heidi's husband was searching the streets of Great Yarmouth with his brother. He walked past her unknowing, and undetected by her, until his brother said softly,

'Jack. Look. She's here.'

·⁂·

As she visibly growled and stared wild-eyed, it did cross Jack's mind to just walk away instead of coaxing her back. If he reclaimed her, she would be his responsibility and the odds of her being his Heidi again didn't look good. But she had left a hole in their lives and wasn't she once all that he needed? They shared a connection through their inability to verbalise the internal isolation they both felt. Whilst he could deflect his own pain, by absorbing himself yet deeper in work, he couldn't deny that this invisible thread was one that bonded him to Heidi, as strong as a rope, and duty screamed loudly in his head.

The disbelief left in her wake had turned to fury and then despondency, the traumatic pain clearly visible in her abandoned children's behaviour, and Jack's confusion and grief scorched him as he owned he had never truly understood her. Living together had never felt as happy as he had hoped it might, but it was what he had witnessed in his own parent's relationship, so he presumed it was enough. They too had their endless weeks of wordless communication and side-stepped each other rather than breezing a waltzed marriage dance.

He had given her everything she could possibly need. His salary enabled her to stay home with the kids, and her car, a stylish convertible in her favourite green, gave her the freedom to get out of the house. He'd never got uptight when her wine budget grew or mentioned the increase of empties, blatantly stacked by the backdoor; as if pleading for his attention. He remembered turning away from the evidence that all was not well.

Heidi's quiet times he'd put down to exhaustion with their children so young. And she'd always been quiet. Remembering how he'd watched her from their bedroom window only two nights before she left, as she stood in the garden barely dressed, gazing at the moon; he had presumed she needed alone time and appreciated how at one she was with nature.

A spell of psychiatric care was deemed the safest way to proceed, and hope was put into her hospitalisation. As Jack looked around the clinical setting a smile broke his habitual frown, 'The NHS can fix everything, can't they? They have magic wands.'

But his voice wasn't as convincing as the words that he chose and as days saw little change, he despairingly said, 'How can a drug not yet be invented that will make everything right?'

He had imagined her soon restored to her position as mother and wife, 'What does she mean when she doesn't respond? When her eyes swim in darkness and her mouth forms no words?'

'Show her the children, Love. Just bring them in,' was the advice from Jack's parents.

Heidi's mother looked doubtful, as she tutted and swayed ever closer to the open door, which exited this scene, 'She was always hard work; it has to be said. We never could read her,' she reluctantly gave. 'Nothing like her sisters. Don't know what's wrong with her but she never would talk to us. Kept us locked out.'

'I wish I could reach her, but she seems too long lost to me now.' Jack's weary, red-eyes desperately wanting to see the return of his once predictable life.

'You're all she ever wanted, Jack, but it still wasn't enough. All her previous failed relationships with their dramatic endings! Attention is what she craves…always has. Maybe if we all just ignore her, she'll come back to you once she's bored,' her mother's advice bitterly landing like a grenade.

'I think she needs us more now than ever,' Jack had said, ignoring the blow but sounding terrified at the prospect of having to dig inside his own hidden self and produce something 'more'.

'How you've stayed loyal, I'll never know! She's kept so much from you. Fancy not knowing she was on anti-depressants before she had the kids. How didn't you see them? Shows how secretive she is.'

'Good God! For a mother, you're something else. I wouldn't want you as my enemy, Doreen.'

⁂

SHE WAS ONLY in the hospital for a week. Discharged to community care, she re-entered her marriage with a drugged, empty stare. She touched each worktop, the hob, and the dish washer, resting her ear against the hum of the fridge. She walked around the sofa, circling it ten times before she folded herself onto the rug with its deep cranberry pile.

'Depression has many branches but there's no need to worry,' the nurse said to calm Jack's anxious, questioning look. 'House life will be so different for Heidi, after being on the streets. Time and the medication we've prescribed will work wonders; you'll see.' Her words were left hanging as she exited their story, with a click of their gate and her car door firmly shut.

But within a few days, an opportunity to escape her containment came. Jack, thinking her too dopy to go, took the children to the park on his last day of compassionate leave. Heidi scarpered, not able to put many miles between them but finding places to hide that not many would know.

Her nose twitched the air as if she was smelling for the first time again; as if fresh bread and spring were floating past her nostrils, enticing her to follow away from the roads. And a look of captivated wonder flashed so brightly as she stretched under the sun. She stroked her arms in marvel at the fur that she felt. This is what she was born to be, at last now she knew.

In her mind, she leapt on long, powerful hind legs. She imagined her coat of mottled brown pelt. She rummaged through long grass, on all fours she circled before resting in shafts of gentle, autumn light. Hidden in the shelter of grass tussocks she whispered 'I'm home' to the breeze that tickled odd ears of corn, perfectly painted against her blue sky. And she knew, in that moment, that this was all she could be and was all she aspired to and all that she felt. All fear and pain lifted and left with the clouds; beyond, to wherever. It didn't matter where to.

RUBY AND PEARL

'*I* never thought Ma would make it to eighty, the way that she coughed,' Pearl told her sister, as she reached over her kitchen table to share the match.

'God, I thought it seemed nothin' could take that battle axe down,' Ruby dragged deeply and then shook her head with the exhale, 'To think a badness grew inside her which finished her off seems ironic, if you think about it. Kind of defeated by her own rotten insides.'

'Well, it's not like cancer's selective. It wasn't like her poisonous soul made a growth appear. Hey, we shouldn't speak ill of her, today of all days. She'll be listening and curse us. Or her Charlie will appear from sneaking behind a wall!'

'Like she hasn't already cursed us...so many times.'

'I think we've done alright, Girl, to show up and do the right thing. Took her grandkids to see her off when they didn't ever really know her, didn't we? I mean, when's the last time your three saw her, Pearl? Apart from passing up town.'

Pearl looked at her children playing in the back with their cousins, as she tried to recall, 'Can't remember. Been years. Maybe it was when Jasper got out last time and he wanted us all round. Do you remember? You couldn't go.'

Ruby nods briefly; she does remember that day. She'd lied, to avoid having to celebrate with their stepfamily that her baby brother Jasper had eagerly claimed as his own.

'It was good to invite Karen over with the kids. I'm surprised she came with us, but I'm glad they're here. Maybe something can regrow out of all of the cracks? The cousins haven't got together in so long, with Jasper away again,' Ruby stands at the kitchen window watching them chase around, the old sandpit now a long jump and the washing line a skipping rope. She watches her Bob, the same age as Jasper's Paul and wonders if they'd be friends if they saw each other regularly. Sadly, she turns back to her sister,

'Mum would turn in her grave knowing what all her boys have become.'

'Oh, come on, Rubes. The writing was on the wall. Charlie had been in and out by the time all the boys were born. Mum knew what she'd got into, from the moment her heart went bang.'

'Hush up. Karen's comin' in. Wouldn't want Jasper hearing about anything we've said. Hi, Love. Take a seat. I'll make another brew.'

'That's such a mum thing to say, ain't it Rubes? Do you remember how she still said samwiches and...'

Ruby breaks into her sister's reflective fast, spluttering on her gulp of tea as she laughs, 'Oh, like you don't, Pearl! You sound more East End than her sometimes, I swear!'

'Do you think your mum ever missed London? Did she ever go back?' Their sister-in-law's voice takes them by surprise as they so seldom hear it. It's quite a gentle voice, which doesn't sit well with the hardness of her face and the way they know she disciplines her kids.

Passing her a mug of tea, and sugar to add herself, Ruby settles at the table again to think on what her sister-in-law has asked,

'Do you know, I don't know. But she never went back. It must have been strange to up sticks after the war like that. But her sister was already settled here, and I suppose that must have helped. I think that's why she came, cause those two were real tight. She would 'ave needed Brenda to lean on with us three being so little and dad just dead.

'They're the kind of things you'd think to ask now, but we was still quite young when she died. I was twenty and you had just turned eighteen, hadn't ya Pearl?'

'Why didn't you two take Jaz with you then? How come he stayed with Ma?'

'Didn't you ever ask him that, Love? Don't you ever talk about these things?'

Karen looks bemused to think that they might have, and the sisters acknowledge once again that conversation in any Marrs family would have excluded them.

'He only ever wanted to be with his stepbrothers, Karen. That's the way it was,' Pearl stepped in for Ruby, as she knew this place was hard. The wound her elder sister bore; the guilt, although misplaced she knew, at not managing to change the path of their brother's life, 'He'd thump me if he heard me refer to them as 'step' brothers, too.'

'Oh, yeh! That makes sense. Those lads are as thick as thieves!' Then, instantly realising a truer word had never been spoken than in the phrase she'd picked, Karen burst out laughing while Ruby looked to Pearl with a sickened stare of disbelief.

Pearl, the middle child, the mediator of all fallouts, stepped in to hang new words like sheets on a waiting line,

'Mum used to reminisce sometimes about how things were when she first moved down. At first, she stayed in Upwell and squeezed in with Brenda's family. She said they only had one room each but did have a kitchen in the back. Remember how scared we were those first nights, Ruby? It was so dark and quiet, after the city. They're my earliest memories, I think, 'cause I was only five. I'll never forget how the fire stayed lit day and night cause that was all there was to keep the damp out and it was so cold.'

'Yeah, I don't forget those things, Pearl. And the name-calling at school. It didn't take long to sort that out though, not after the boxing rings were rigged up. Londoners against Locals; the boys, not the girls. But we got into scraps sometimes too, just to establish ourselves. Then mum would get in such a rage, 'I'm not havin' my gals raised in no gutter!' she'd rant. She always wanted us to be like princesses or something. Remember how persnickety she was about our hair, Pearl? I don't know where that came from. But I'm grateful to her for looking out for us and bringing us up different to her boys.'

A silent gap spread over the table creating an invisible divide, which again separated the sisters from their sister-in-law, although it wasn't their intention.

'It's good how you took on that boy,' Karen said over her shoulder to Ruby, as she emptied her dregs in the sink. 'Is he about Paul's age?'

'Yeh, that's right. They're all pretty close in age really, aren't they? Pearl's Lucy is nine like your Julie. It's a shame they don't see more of each other really. You know you can come over whenever you like, Karen?'

'It's hard, with not drivin'. And you know Jaz don't like it so much. It's a shame you three don't get on anymore.'

The sisters both nod but they had to resign themselves long ago to the decisions Jasper made when holding so tightly to his stepfather's family and disowning what he saw as snobby sisters who thought themselves better than the Marrs. The imminent split had fractured completely when the sisters had chosen to keep their own father's name; reverting from Marrs to Stones when their mother had passed, as they had never been part of that blood.

'He had choices. He could have moved in with us, but he went with his brothers to stay with Ma,' Ruby's voice left her more defensively than she had meant, and she walked over to put the kettle on out of habit.

'So how old was Bob, when you adopted him, Ruby?' The younger woman seemed intrigued with this part of her sister-in-law's life.

'He was almost one. He had two sisters, but my Harry said the only kid he'd have would be a boy. They all went different ways and that near broke my heart. His oldest sister, Sonia, was a bright little thing. She'd cuddle up right close to you and need a lot of love. But the younger girl was distant and much more hard work. I often wonder where they are now.'

'Well, you worry too, don't ya Rube?...in case one of them turns up here looking for him in a few years' time,' Pearl shared honestly.

'Well, why d'ya let that bother ya? Be good, wouldn't it? If they all got together again one day.' Ruby snapped a sharp look in reply to Karen's innocent question,

'No, it bloody wouldn't. Bob doesn't know he's adopted. Would do him no good to know. It's hard enough for him to feel secure with Harry often such a ...' Ruby hushed her words in time, with her husband just in the next-door room.

'What?' Karen's insistence to uncover the most secretive part of Ruby's life was becoming bothersome and most uninvited. She hardly knew the woman and she was getting all personal,

'It's complicated,' Ruby whispered roughly, indicating the conversation was at its end, 'for everyone. Somethings are just best left alone.'

'Oh, bloody hell! Talk about complicated!' The fear and panic expressed in Karen's remark had Pearl and Ruby snap their heads round sharp to follow her gaze out into the back garden. There, like a terrier after rabbits, strode wide-shouldered Adam, one of their three half-brothers and Ma's favourite grandson. They watched frozen for a minute as he grabbed at Karen's kids and the sisters noticed how Karen retreated and, rather than challenge him, hid.

'It's alright, Love. You're fine. You've done nothin' wrong...' but Pearl's words were ended by the backdoor being kicked open once the handle was down and the two terrified children being shoved in the room,

'What the fuck are ya doin' here, you stupid bitch? What will Jez say, when I tell him 'bout this? Like ya hang out with them on the day she's put in the ground. Of all the places to come. Bloody cow, that's what ya are.' His words were replaced with a slap that stung the room as Karen's cheek burned. Ruby instinctively pulled the children to her and stroked their small heads whilst trying to turn their faces to her tummy, to block out the scene. She felt the fight in the boy, as he threw her off and looked torn between loyalties to his mother or uncle. Pearl barred the door from the other children trying to get in.

'What ya doin' in my kitchen?' came the timely boom from Pearl's Harry. Stood in the doorway, it was clear he'd been roused from a nap, with his hair all anyhow and his usual sharp eyes still looking blurry.

'I've come to get this lot out of here, ain't I. Like I'd be in here otherwise!' He spat on the floor.

Harry moved closer but the sisters understood his constraint. It wasn't until Adam shoved Ruby into her spinner, while pulling back the kids, that Harry's temper completely broke and he threw a punch that Adam dodged, like the fighter that he was,

'Don't be startin' something ya can't get out of. Do ya really wanna bring it on? Just you an' all of us? Thought not, you fuckin' losers. Get in the car. Now.' Karen and her children scampered out like their feet were on fire. Adam's look was thunder but his breathing undisturbed; although he moved like a bull, he was as controlled and deliberate as a deadly snake.

'You all had no right being at her funeral today. Her next door is more Marrs than you lot, but even she knew to keep away,' were his parting words.

'You and your bloody family!' Harry said, as he retreated once more to the sitting room, 'make us a bloody cuppa tea.'

For a moment Pearl and Ruby let the new silence bathe them. They took opposite seats, and both folded their hands identically on the pretty flowered tablecloth. Heavy bosoms expanded with deep inhales and rested once more on the table top in each released sigh. When Ruby realised they had both started to trace round the design's shapes with their fore fingers, she puzzled whether their habits would be so identical if they lived countries apart, or had they been mirrored by their close proximity. She laughed to point it out,

'Family's a funny thing, ain't it? Blood thicker than water, and all that. Jasper couldn't be further cut from our cloth, could he? Do you see any of mum in him, Pearl?' She passes her younger sister a cigarette and stands to make Harry's long-awaited cuppa.

'A lot of it was how Charlie made them, weren't it? Having them fight each other and having boxing more important than any book work. He bred them to fight, let's face it. Their training ground the fairs and school yards. I used to think it must have broken mum's heart to have her boys reared like that but it's like that's how she thought it should be. The stealing was something else, of course. She wouldn't 'ave wanted them to follow Charlie's 'career but she must 'ave known that's how it would turn out. He was such an influence on them all.'

'And on her,' Ruby recalls as she sits back down to tap her fag on the ashtray between them. 'God, she loved him like crazy though, didn't she? I used to think she'd abandon us if he'd asked her to. But it always felt a bit like that anyway, even though we all shared a house. I think that's why I wanted to help Bob so, I mean apart from not being able to have our own kids. I felt so much empathy for those three little lost souls. Wanted to make everything safe for them. See them alright.'

'Here, Rubes, take this,' Pearl offered her hanky for her sister's rare tears and moved closer to rub on her back,

'We've done alright, Girl, you and me. And we're determined our children will get educated and see the value in that, so they'll make different paths and not just tread water or stay stranded on the dirt.'

'Well, Bob's not doing so well with ol' school, Pearl. He's full of tricks for the teachers, and cheek. That's what gets Harry so mental; when the boy always mouths back. He's a world champion wind-up artist...honest, you can't ever get the last word.'

'But he's a loving boy, ain't he? And isn't that worth a lot? Look at them playing again. I hope they've not got affected by that little scene. I should go have a word with them.'

'Call them in, Pearl. It's time they got some tea.' Ruby returned to the steaming kettle and poured into three mugs, 'I'll do them something quick before you have to go. What time's Tony in? Or did you say he was working nights?'

'Yeh, this week's nights. And that's another reason I was glad to be out of the house today. He gets so down...yeh, even worse...when he's doing nights.'

'I never understand why he doesn't look for something else. Especially when he didn't get the foreman job he wanted so bad.'

'I think it's a lack of self-confidence. Can't really think why else. I've asked enough times. But I've got my Tupperware parties to keep me busy and out of his hair…and the kids. Yeah, thank God, we have them. There's nothin' much else glues us these days, it has to be said.' Moving to the back door, while Ruby scans her cupboard for beans, Pearl calls the cousins in and starts laying the table,

'What ya got there, Bob?' she asks, noticing he is cradling something in his hands as he walks in to join the rest.

'It's a fallen chick. Look, Mum,' he says as Ruby returns from the sitting room looking a little harassed, 'I think it's one of those long-tailed tits from my book. Look at its colours. I found it just now, down by the hedge. Can we save it?'

His cousins clamber round to take a look; the older boys soon sitting down, not very impressed and hopeful of food, but Lucy stays staring at the tiny form,

'It's so beautiful. I've never seen a bird like it. Look how long its tail is, Mum.'

'Oh, Bob! That can't survive. Look how tiny it is,' Ruby warns. 'Best thing you can do is to smack a spade on it. Really, Love.' Although Ruby attempted some kindness in her too-honest words, she failed miserably. Saddened to think of the pain this little bird's imminent death will bring to her son, her manner becomes irritable rather than warm,

'Look, I'll empty a bucket and you can make it a nest but don't get attached, Bob. They never survive when they're so young. We can't rear it the same as its mum, can we?'

'But it's worth a try, isn't it, Mum?' And his eyes are so honest and radiant of hope that she feels something shift

136

inside her and an intense pride and love so overwhelming brings a tear to her eye. These are the feelings she should of course share, but she stuffs them down quickly because her life's edges are sharp and she's no good at the soft stuff, although she wishes she were.

FEN ROADS

*D*o you get tired of ghost stories always being set in one type of weather? The hazy mist of winter, when exhaled breath is held in the air and the freeze is as external as the internally caused fear? The skeletal trees' branches snagging and taking the shape of phantom terror? But, then again, there is often a thunderstorm, with cracks of lightening that uncovers what may or may not be there, often accompanied by an oppressive heat, a foreboding tension that the weather too may be in on the haunting.

The weather held no such drama that morning, as the girl sat in her usual seat on the bus. It never occurred to her to question how she was always the first passenger to board the bus and secure her window spot; first on the right of the forward-facing seats. Lost in her teenage memories and reflecting on far less pragmatic concerns, the weather did manage to catch her attention. It was almost the turn of the season, but February clung to its bitterest reputation, with sharpened talons and shrieks of defiance, terrifying any glimpse of shine away.

It was extremely cold, but what her father would have called 'fresh'. The sky had a subtle suggestion of ice blue shyly mingling with the more general grey wash. The clouds so wide they showed no character or menace; more a gigantic, flat sheet with no mountainous suggestion or herringbone breaks. Not yet midday, the sun had already lost its battle with its rays too weak. Spring's promise lay hidden under winter mud and the nights that arrived too early.

The lack of event, reflected in this landscape, matched that of the girl's spirit. Weary but not quite lethargic, listless, and yet far from comatose; as unremarkable as the four-teen-mile journey that lay ahead, connecting Wisbech to Kings Lynn. The main path of the journey, the laboriously straight A47, cut through fen fields like one of their manmade dykes. Scar upon scar in the land's canvas.

This ride had been the girl's Saturday ritual since knowing her friend Lucy. With Lucy's mum, they had always gone to Lynn on a Saturday afternoon, and later, with Lucy's eldest brother, driven back for the KFC Saturday evening treat. But they'd moved away, and the girl, too young to drive, replaced the comfort and company of those trips with a diesel sighing bus, changing gears as if resentful for the work. What did it imagine was its destiny? She smiled to herself at her fanciful thoughts of the dirty vehicle polished and sipping cocktails from a sun lounger.

The sky kept calling her thoughts back to it; the space always pulling, tricking: today it felt ever sharper in its draw. A fen sky is bigger, as large as they come. How this statement of her father's drove her crazy as a child. He, a painter, loved East Anglia for it. He could see lines of colour; many, many variations in the bleak backdrop he was inspired by. She despised it. The lack of contrast between earth, sky, and water. The ugly, gaping, silt-sided rivers, boringly straight, as if lacking any story or secret. How she wished to escape this landscape of her birth. And yet, here she stayed. Waiting.

At the Horse Fair bus station, passengers piled on and the girl patted the seat beside her, indicating to a worn-looking mother to take it. As always, she was ignored, and the mother walked past without any acknowledgement. Only her toddler's wide grin and observant eyes smiled at the girl, as she wiggled in her mother's arms and blew a gurgled bubble. The little one seemed amused to be carried so pink and Queen-like, while her throne was lifted on by the driver. Why everyone avoided the empty seat next to the girl was a mystery that she had no time for. It was of no concern.

An old woman stamped her feet as she climbed on, dramatically indicating the presence of both herself and the weather. Dressed in an unusual mixture of black lace and tasselly shawl, her long, tired hair had an abandoned look, giving the impression of an ancient Romani crossed with Stevie Nicks in disarray. She caught the girl's eye and saw her surprise that such a flowing skirt should fall to meet heavy Doc Martins. The old woman declared to all, as if in answer,

'If ya feet is cold, ya whole body's cold!'

A Fen localism, as age-old as the clay clods that re-form with each rain; but spoken with a heavy hint of cockney. Her voice had a clarity that gave each word emphasis and deliberation. It was surprisingly loud for someone whose frailty had her grasping for support as she moved into the bus.

A fellow old age pensioner, opposite the girl's seat, caught the woman's arm as she passed and, telling her to 'hold yew hard,' made room for her beside him. The two became engrossed in weather talk, as she peeled her dainty black lace gloves from her small white hands. They looked almost translucent, so delicately placed in her lap. And much in contrast with the reality of her voice and boots.

'Well, yew know what thay say abowt March, doin't yew? She comes in like a lion and goes out like a lamb,' the old man's chest rattled, as he chuckled at his own idiom.

An annoying squirt of a dog sniffed and growled as he was jerked past these front seats to sit further back. Thinking it was a reaction to the toddler's thrust hand, excitedly thrown down in search of a stroke, the owner warned the mother,

'He'll 'ave 'er. Mind owt.'

The girl turned to look out the window but, intrigued by the old pair, covertly watched their reflections in the glass. There was something that this woman had brought with her. Onto the bus. But the girl couldn't yet decipher the energy and what it meant. She was confused by the colours of it. What it might bring.

As the familiar route began its straight stretch, the girl watched the detached house come into sight on her left. A wide field's distance from the road, she imagined it before the main artery was created to link the two towns. Would the house have stood more isolated still? More apparent on the barren, flat fen fields? Or would this route have always been well trodden; by horse and cart, by galloping gentlemen and lolloping farmers? An old nursery rhyme surfaced but wasn't enough to break her tension. As she turned her head to catch the last image of the disappearing house, she realised again that she had been holding her breath. Clenching her jaw. Tightening her shoulders.

Feeling self-aware, she hurriedly raised her eyes to the couple's reflection, checking they hadn't observed her. Curiously, she could hardly make out the woman's image and rubbed at the window to wipe the gathering condensation. It must be my breath she considered, enjoying that the buses reluctant heating system was finally having some effect on her cold bones. As she cleared a circle, she saw the old woman's eyes were fixed directly on her own, with a strange expression on her face. The telling lips were almost smiling but too knowingly to be a neighbourly gesture, rather delivering a very invasive and piercing knowledge. The girl instantly felt uncomfortable; sweat prickled on her palms, her breath felt caught and sharp.

With no rustle of bags, no 'excuse me' or unsteady gangway step, the old woman moved seamlessly next to her. Nestling in far too close and leaning to her ear, with the undertone of a confidante, she whispered,

'Do ya wanna to talk about it?'

Her breath was stale with the linger of ketones. Her fingers yellowed. The girl internally recoiled. There was an fiercing draught that surrounded her arrival and the girl shuddered. Was it spiteful? She felt the bleakness of the day return to her legs; her jeans material too inadequate for the penetrating freeze.

A gape was all she could manage in her shock, that the old woman had not only noticed her but also moved to her side.

'I see ya. The way ya looked at it. It means sumin' to ya, don't it?' The woman's rattled breath sounded deep and desperate, leaving her words drowning in the bubble of her lungs. No longer strong but certain in their need to be heard.

The girl steadied herself, as much as she could. There was a pounding in her ears but, in her confusion, she wasn't clear if it could be her blood beating too hard. This woman would have been called an old pikey, if at the girl's primary school gates; she imagined her next move would be to get her heather out to sell, or lavender from Norfolk. Feeling deeply uncomfortable, caught out, and exposed, the girl panicked that her mind could be read by such a woman. And yet, suddenly there was an unexpectedly welcome and poignant warmth exuding from those same brittle bones. Her bony hip touched the girl's, leaving a strangely reassuring comfort.

'Ya travel this road a lot, don't ya?' Her question was rhetorical, and her clear eyes twinkled like a cat who knows it has cornered its mouse, 'stuck on fen roads ain't ya?'

'What do you want?' The girl's voice was much more a whisper than she had intended. She had wanted the woman to be scared and move away. And yet, she wanted her to stay close. To stay with her.

Her neighbour smiled that odd half smile again. The wrinkles that puckered around her mouth stretched enough to show some of her stained teeth,

'Just thought ya might wanna talk about it.' Seeing the girl's reticent expression, she added, 'About the house. About what happened. Maybe I need a 'why' before...' She twisted her mouth, looking down whilst rubbing one boot against the other, 'And I've no particular place to go.' She added the last phrase in a peculiar, almost sung voice. Creepy in its subtlety. It reminded the girl of some song

Lucy would repeat over and over and she felt memories being pulled from her, as if on an invisible yarn. She considered the woman's homemade shawl and imagined her deliberately chosen words like a crochet hook, plunging to retrieve the stitch needed to continue the story.

The girl looked to her hands, trying to ground herself. Trying to appreciate what was occurring. Concentrate on your nail varnish, she willed herself but, filled with shame at the scruffy age of it, she snapped her eyes back to the woman's. It was so surreal but if she wanted to know, to listen, could she talk about it? Would it be good to? She tried her voice again, the 'hmm' sounded stronger. Maybe she could do this?

Glancing around, it was as if no-one else had noticed them. Everyone's head seemed bowed, fiddling with something in their laps, or cajoling children to sit still or, just a few, pre-occupied in conversation. The woman's abandoned passenger was now snoring in fits, as his head bobbed in time with the buses jerking movements.

'I've reached my end. I won't tell any living souls!' the old woman continued to encourage, laughing with wheezy breaths, 'It's fun to be so reliable at this end of the game!'

'I've not talked about it before. I don't know where to start.' The girl's honesty made her appear child-like, 'I'm not sure how to tell it.' But the older woman's demeanour seemed increasingly familiar and accepting in her encouragement. Safe.

'The beginning may be lost to you. Ignore the stepping-stones of time. You don't need those now. Just recall the night itself.'

The girl puzzled the passenger's words. They seemed like a riddle, and she'd never been able to concentrate hard enough on those. Always too lazy to push boxes in her mind out of the way and seek much further back, into the lesser-used corners of her brain to explore for the correct answers. But, yeah. She knew that night. That bit was sharp. Easily retrieved.

'It was a Saturday. Like any other…' she bravely began, checking which emotion was being shown in the woman's eyes constantly. 'Well, since Lucy and I had become such inseparable friends. I'd sleep over every weekend, never stopping to think what her family thought. Whether I was an inconvenience. Expensive addition too, as they always treated me. I never heard them grumble. Never thought to ask for money from my parents.' She added this with some shame. Some knowledge surfacing that she had been self-absorbed to always presume they would pay for her, too; 'You don't think of anyone other than yourself really, do you? When you're fourteen.' She regarded her companion's aged face and wondered if those years could be recalled. They were like yesterday to her.

'That was her house. The one we passed when you caught me looking. But it's like you already know that?' She searched the woman's face harder, deeper, for some explanation but her steady eyes only expressed patient waiting. She wanted to hear more. 'Do I know you?'

As if the woman had heard her silent question, she lifted a feathery hand to the girl's face. Abruptly, it was avoided with a toss of fiery hair and swiftly crossed legs. The old woman would have to tell the girl who she was first. Why she was so intrigued by her. 'Go on,' the elder encouraged, with a hint of plea in her china-blue eyes.

'There was nothing much to do. We would lie around listening to our records, have some Malibu or whatever else we got our hands on. When Lucy's mum, Pearl, said we could go into Lynn with her it seemed exciting. Well, as in it varied the pattern. So that became our habit. Then Gary, her brother, said we could go with him to pick up the KFC in the evening and life positively shone! Kings Lynn had a KFC! We were getting out on trips! Like two Labradors excitedly clambering into the back of the car, tails wagging and eagerly obedient so as not to get uninvited. I would have been a Red Setter, actually, with my auburn hair and skinny build, but Lucy could have been an ever-faithful golden Lab!' The girl suddenly stopped, surprised at the realisation that she was happy. Talking had opened a drawer packed full of dear and cherished memories. She could see that the woman was enjoying her recollections too, so much so that her eyes had become shiny with…could it be tears?

'There was always something about Lucy's dad, but I didn't know what. I think he must have been depressed. He would sit quietly, always in the same armchair, watching telly. He didn't contribute much to anything, while Pearl was like the entertainment. Her croaky London voice, ridiculously youthful energy, and cackle of a laugh. She would smoke these mini cigar-like cigarettes. We couldn't nick them 'cause they tasted so weird! She smoked way too much, too,' she added, nodding in recognition of her neighbour's wheezing chest. She wondered why she hadn't lit up yet. Everyone smokes on these buses, don't they? Whipping her head round to see if anyone was, there was only the nauseating smell of the bus seat material on the no-doubt filthy head rests.

'So, it was a Saturday night. Malibu and our favourite tunes absorbed, Lucy and I left as if on our way to London, not King's Lynn! We didn't dress up though. Lucy hated all that show, although she loved David Sylvian. He could get away with using black eyeliner! Lucy admired his artistry. Have you heard of him? Lead singer of Japan.'

The old woman's eerie singing started again, tugging another familiar thread from way back, 'When my chance came to begin…'

'The ghosts of my life blew wilder than the wind.' They both whispered the line together, both stretching the 'wind' as Japan's haunting recording had done.

'Ghosts.' The woman's eyes fixed the girl's, with the stamp of her word. A heartbeat missed. A moment suspended. 'You do know you are one?'

The girl's knotted brow looked torn between denial and acceptance. So strange that this woman should know the name of that song. Know so much. But everything around them seemed so unreal. Lost in time. Flustered, the girl wrestled the improbability that someone so old, so different, could know these lyrics and demand such an agonising question of her. She fought images in her mind to find hesitant words,

'Is that why no one sees me? But you do…'

'Yes. Like I said, my time's at an end. I'll be passing any day now. That's why I can see ya.'

'And you're not scared? Terrified? To die.'

'No. Not at all. I want to be back with my children.'

The girl swallowed back bile at the woman's words. A sadness swept over her with such weight that she was knocked back in her seat, crumpled. Suddenly, remembering the toddler, she sat bolt upright in terror,

'So, the little one's to be taken too? She seems to see me. Is that what you're saying?'

'No. No, Love. Little ones can see things that get missed as we grow up. She won't be able to remember that she saw ya, and in a few more months she'll have lost the gift too.'

'Is it a gift? To see the dead?' She realised she was chipping at the already wrecked pink ends of her fingers, jabbing at her cuticles. Internally tearing this conversation away, she returned to her story, 'We were jeans-and-T-shirt girls. It was hot. Yeah, it was summer.' She was lost for a moment, but time allowed it for her. No pressure to tell. Not like standing in class and having a minute to explain an idea or read your given passage in English class.

'Gary was very sensible and seemed so grown-up. I mean, he was only seventeen and had paid for his own driving lessons. Passed his test. So responsible...he was like an extra dad! He had a girlfriend who was going to Uni to be a dietician. Yeah, he was smart. Well, Lucy was too. I was a hanger-on. A whisper. A candle in the wind, to quote Elton.' She smiled shyly, aware she had exposed too much of herself. Changing the focus from her detour, she added, 'Yeah, that couple had purpose and Lucy would have found some, too.' The words came easily with this woman feeling like a friend. Increasingly she felt like she knew her. She became sure she must have known her once. Read-justing her position, the girl wriggled in her seat and stretched her legs out as much as possible.

'Go on,' the woman coaxed again, her gentler tone reflected a wisdom of equal surprise, 'Don't get stuck at the reflective. Tell it like it was. I need to know, don't I.' The girl couldn't let go of this woman's eyes for some time. She sat there, frozen to them, as an awareness began to trickle through the damaged scenes of her mind, dancing with the memories and joining fragments to complete the picture. The old woman's eyes bored into her, and yet through her.

They wanted too much; they were the windows to a pain so real, so fresh, that the girl felt panic at the thought of what lay ahead. But the now familiar gravelly voice wrapped itself around her and made her feel home.

'I've tried to get through before, Pearl. I wanted to help with your pain,' the girl's desperate speech was weak; ashamed in her inability to reach Lucy's mum many years earlier. But, with the realisation that she could now give what the woman desperately needed to know, an instant surge of peace overrode her fear. A realisation that she too could leave by this door, she too could rest, if she could do this one small favour for a fractured soul. It no longer felt uncomfortable, impossible. The girl was no longer scared. She was confronting her shame.

'The radio's on. We're being daft in the back of the car… me and Lucy. We're on our way back to hers with the food. It smells so good but I'm having a thick, indulgent milk-shake and beginning to feel awful queasy. I think I'll puke. Yeah, definitely. It's the Malibu and the car's motion. I'm not used to cars much….my parents don't drive.

'But Gary's so proud of his car. Oh God! This is so embarrassing. Lucy's laughing as she tries to wind the window down and move the KFC bucket well away from me. Gary hears the commotion, 'What are you two up to? Hey…' as he sees me heaving into my lap, 'Christ's sakes, Lucy! Deal with her. Not in my car.'

"Look at the road! I've got this,' Lucy shouted back, suddenly panicked at how mad he'll be. Knowing our Saturday KFC trips are over. Maybe her relationship with her 'far-too-mature for us' brother, too.'

The girl's memory makes her as nauseous now, as she was then. The sway in her stomach and the swirl in her head are gathering momentum…rising, pushing, 'Oh, Christ!' she shouts too loudly but no longer cares who on the bus may hear. She is totally absorbed in the moment that she can see in her head,

'But he can't keep his eyes on the road! His car pride is bigger than his driving experience, and he's looking back far too much. For far…too…long. For…' each word is swallowed in her anxious saliva, that races through her mouth suffocating her short, panicky breath. She's gasping. Gulping air.

'I don't hear the crash. The metal smash metal.' Breathe. Breathe.

'The screeching and clashing. The thudding and scraping. The hissing and yanking. I don't hear any screaming. Any gurgling or whimper.' Breathe. Slow down. Slow down.

'I can't see the lights. Flashing. Bleeping through stillness. The postures. The expressions. The smells of burnt rubber. Petrol. Blood. Summer tarmac is by my nose.'

There's silence. As if the world has stopped. No more beating in her ears. She feels alone but knows she's still here on the bus. Still waiting.

So lost in that moment, the girl missed seeing Pearl Stone clutch at her heart and fall from her seat. She only became aware of the scene around her as passengers' ran to help the woman; desperately attempting to bring back life. The diesel induced drone of the bus engine cutting out; the driver grabbing his resus kit.

'It was here, weren't it?' Another rhetorical question breaks the quiet in the girl's head. Spoken from the woman's soul, which is rapidly leaving her finished life, 'Right here, on this bit of the road.'

Can't they see that the old woman has left? Can't they see her soul flutter past the toddler, in playful delight; baby hands stretching as if trying to catch bubbles.

The girl sees herself become indiscernible. Her hands look to fade from her lap. Her lap is clouded in a haze. Is it her own eye's that fail her, that she must now leave behind? She can see through herself, to the pack of cigarellas that must have slipped from Pearl's bag and were under her leg all the time.

'The three of you did die outright, didn't you?' Again, the woman's voice sounds desperate, and yet kind. Soft. Forgiving. The girl floats above the woman's rising presence. Stretches her form to take the other one in, caressing her with her gently replied, 'Yes. Yes. It was instant.'

The bus fades away from them. It is irrelevant. Only the woman's shell stays on it. The two souls are above the road. Lost from sight. Back to where this journey always takes the girl. Where it always ends.

'Fank ya, love. I needed to have the 'why'. I needed to be sure they knew no pain. I'm at peace now. And you can stop your restless years of journeying the same road.' Pearl's voice connects through an awareness. Spoken not by mouth but by particles unseen by an eye. Her deep despair is mixed with a blessed finality which drifts her like a peaceful wave to rest.

'Can you forgive me?'

Pearl's 'yes' is layered in warmth and affection. A small but profound kiss of acceptance. The girl realises she is suspended in this same timeless wonder. She belongs to no time. She can let go.

'Why do ya start in Wisbech an' not from our house?'
Pearl's voice comes through the airwaves. It's crackling,
disappearing. Seeping into the girl from far above.

''Cause, that's where I'm from. That's where I lived,' she
corrects herself, swooping within the wind, mounting
higher and further than she has ever been. The wisps of
someplace else build up around her and carry her
forwards, across and away from the Fen.

Character Tree

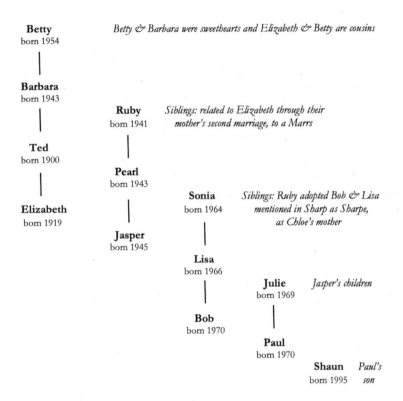

Betty
born 1954

Betty & Barbara were sweethearts and Elizabeth & Betty are cousins

Barbara
born 1943

Ruby
born 1941

Siblings: related to Elizabeth through their mother's second marriage, to a Marrs

Ted
born 1900

Pearl
born 1943

Elizabeth
born 1919

Sonia
born 1964

Siblings: Ruby adopted Bob & Lisa mentioned in Sharp as Sharpe, as Chloe's mother

Jasper
born 1945

Lisa
born 1966

Julie
born 1969

Jasper's children

Bob
born 1970

Paul
born 1970

Shaun
born 1995

Paul's son

Shaun's girlfriend (Clare) is related to The Leveret's Heidi & Pearl is the old lady in Fen Roads

Amsterdam, 1566

'The hog can be smelt from the street for Lord's sake! We must be humble to remain unbothered,' Leivan cries, with his panic barely disguised.

His wife doesn't look at him as she raises her hand in firm dismissal. 'No. On this, I am sure. I will not sneak from my land like an injured dog, unmissed and as if we were banished. For once, I am unafraid.'

'Then you are a fool, Barbel!' Leivan coughs, as he tries to lower his voice whilst conveying his anger, 'What use is our freedom when we are burning at stakes?'

It is too much for the excited and pre-occupied woman. She rushes to him with her finger to her mouth and burning eyes, 'Hush now. No more. A feast is ready and our guests arrive as we speak. Let us join them and cherish this last supper together. They look for those Protestants that revolt in the streets, not families having friends to dinner. Come, Anna,' she turns to the young servant, who is worriedly wiping her hands on her apron, 'I am sure that the pies have had time. Get them out and bring up more wine.'

'Mother, I am sorry if I kept you,' says their daughter, Mariss, as she floats in without care. Her skirt brushes the tabletop and she dusts flour from the linen. 'Packing has near tired me out! A drink is required please, dear Anna, if I am to be of any company this day.'

Mariss goes to her father and gently takes his arm, unaware of the confusion she has caused their young servant who now juggles too many jobs. Mariss smiles so sweetly that Leivan has no choice but to forgive her lateness and plants a kiss on her cheek.

'You look beautiful, my darling,' he says softly, allowing his head a moment of stillness.

Barbel points Mariss to the room above them, in which their guests gather, indicating she should join them. She then instructs Anna to go and tell her son to come down immediately.

Seeing that Anna is becoming flustered, Barbel guides her, 'You can take the wine up as you go.' She turns to Leivan, and speaking more softly, attempts to assure him with her strong, certain words,

'This house has kept us safe through many years of troubled times. Its walls won't fail us now. It is eight months since you witnessed the trouble first-hand but none has been seen here, but that caused by our own faith!'

He knows that she is as afraid as him, especially since the increase in activity of the Beeldenstorm. The mobs of Calvinist supporters continue to wreck the churches and any cathedrals, the monasteries and convents. Little life is lost but rioters tear apart the buildings, set fire to organs and costly works. A child was killed in Amsterdam just last week, accidently hit by the rocks being hurled. Barbel has always been a stoic woman and therefore of good support in times such as this, but Leivan knows she fears the repercussion that shall follow as much as he.

'You weren't there, Barbel, so can never know the scene. You can only hold such repugnant scent in your nose if standing next to charred remains. And it never leaves you but stays fresh in the memory as the moment that it invades your senses.'

'Come, Leivan,' Barbel encourages, still refusing to be drawn into his darkness, 'you should be welcoming our friends, not upsetting about what we cannot change.'

The kitchen is at the rear of the house. The room above it houses their gathering. The deep, narrow merchant's house is perfect for such hidden occasions; only those invited would know of the feast within. Leivan opens the double doors wide as he enters their large entertaining room, mustering his more usual commanding voice, with an air of cheer and full heart,

'Friends, friends, a toast to you all, for we are soon to be parted but you must always know that you are within our hearts.'

Passing from one guest to the other his forced joviality becomes sincere after a short time. He loses himself in the enjoyment of the good wine, company and gentle tunes that the viol and recorder play. He becomes confident enough to leave the double doors open, so that the room to the front of the house is included for their number. He allows a tickle of excitement to mix with all his apprehensions, stored for the change that is now just a week away.

Up, in his higher rooms, Jowan is not yet finished. Head buried under her skirts, he is enjoying his pre-feast and her squeals of delight,

'Jowan, I shall miss you so,' Ren cries, 'and your tongue!'
He brings himself up and upon her before she can protest,
'Not just my tongue I hope!' he smiles, as he thrusts deeply into her.

'You had better pull out sharply,' her voice warns, but

smothered in a buttery delight that is hard to judge, 'I need no forever gift.'

Anna, their house servant, gives a quiet rap on the door and delivers her mistress's command through the wooden divide, 'Excuse me knocking but your mother is becoming fretful that you have not yet come down.' She knows full well what keeps him.

Jowan clamps his hand over the girl's mouth, as her giggles mount, 'Let mother know I am coming,' he calls cheekily, finishing with a groan of deep pleasure.

Ren rolls from him and starts to recover the rest of her clothes from the floor by his bed. She sees his leather recipe book, its open page showing a diagram sketch. She looks at his handwriting and imagines him holding the quill. Pausing and twiddling his hair, as he considers each point he has written, just as he would read a book when younger.

She sits back up and begins to re-dress. 'Seven years it has been since we first met, as helpless as each other and needing to know the ways of it. I still think of you as your fourteen-year-old self, with your tousled, blond hair and blue eyes twinkling like sun on water!'

'You taught me well, as I have for you. We are special to each other, dear Ren. I will miss you too,' Jowan adds, as he swiftly dresses and looks out of the window to his precious canal, where his family's barge patiently awaits them. He goes to her and places a gentle kiss on her fore-head. A tear escapes from her eye and she feels both confused and shame at it.

Jowan places the coins in her hand but she refuses them, 'No, not this time Jowan. These coins could not be spent.'

'Remember to keep your heart hard, Flower. There is no man should make you weep. You will always be my 'Gem of a Ren'', he laughs as he pulls her close, 'Keep your clients limited as you always have. Soldiers would be rough and not pay well, so do not be tempted by their number when they ride in.'

'They will take what they want for no fee apparently. That is what we hear.' Her expression is sorrowful but not weak. Her ability to get by without complaint is one that Jowan admires.

The sweet smell of his kiss, and the realisation that this really is a final goodbye, make Ren turn away, struggling to hide her bared emotions from him. She throws her fiery hair over her face.

'Look at me, Ren,' he holds her chin up, but the girl cannot lift her eyes. 'You are here,' Jowan places his hand on his heart. The gesture makes the girl laugh and smile again as she reminds him, with a casual toss of her hair, 'I would not wish to believe I was the keeper of *your* heart! I pray for any that would believe that!'

Jowan smiles at her. He *will* miss her. She has made him happy. He blows her a kiss as he opens the wooden door, 'Oh! Remember to wait a while. When you can hear the music, it will be safe to pass on the stairs.'

Jowan whistles as he descends the stairs, two at a time and with a playful air. He welcomes the excitement of change and sees adventure in the unknown journey ahead of his family. Peeking his head into the entertaining room he immediately spots Greta, a current flame who will no doubt demand his attention. He doesn't want to approach her straight away so instead he sidles in next to his Aunt, who is in a constant flow of tears.

'Do you believe these tales of murder and rape? The Spanish rule of Flanders to be so vicious in its oppression of the Protestants?'

Jowan finds her exaggerated 'fret' as annoying as her blink-ered outlook,

'We do not upheave ourselves for poor reason, Aunt Gertha. Do you doubt our attachment to Amsterdam?

There are new stories each time we trade. They cannot all be fabricated. I worry about my father's family in Antwerp, presently much closer to the threat than we are.'

'But we are overseen by a Spanish Governor…Margaret of Parma is the Spanish King's half-sister, is she not? And she promises to stop religious repression.'

Jowan has struggled with the same thoughts but, having sought various opinions, is aware that their Spanish Governor's position is vulnerable, 'It's hard to believe such monstrosities happen in the name of religion, but I have witnessed enough to know that it can be so. As tensions mount here, I think you should practise our faith underground.'

'In hindsight, if only my Ivan had taken up the weaving trade. The bookwork has seen us well, but has none of your rewards,' she returns to sniffing and gasping, blowing hard on a kerchief pulled from her sleeve's cuff, 'And now, with you all going far from me, it seems harsher to bear.'

'Aunt…dear aunt. You were offered to come but had no wish in reality. Maybe, once you have heard how well we are settled, you will change your mind and join us?' Jowan tells her gently. She responds with a larger sob than perhaps meant and takes a large gulp of her wine to try and disguise the noise.

Jowan turns to review his situation, accidently catching the eye of the blonde Greta, who watches him attentively from across the room. Her smile is inviting and encourages him over. He kisses her hand, taking the space beside her.

'You have worn my favourite gown, Greta,' smiling as he looks her slowly up and down. She blushes and fiddles with the empty, pewter tankard in her hand. The blue trim, at her neck, highlights her soft, golden curls as they fall over her shoulders. Jowan is charmed by her femininity; her attractiveness further enhanced by the warm glow of the fire.

'You said you could not be here, that we would have no further farewell. What changed your mind?' he teases, delighting that her comfort remains fully disturbed.

'I want for a witty retort, but I can find none today, Jowan. I did not want to come and yet found myself pulled to.'

'I shall return. You know this, Greta. It will take a little time for us to re-establish our business, but I see this happening within a few summers. When trade flourishes, we shall need to travel overseas, thus returning me here.'

Although Jowan smiles reassuringly the girl looks alarmed, 'So, it is only your trade that will call you home? Do you not see any hope for us, Jowan?'

He can see that she is struggling to contain the passion in her voice and, feeling slightly cornered, he declares, 'There is always hope!' gesturing with his arms thrown as widely as possible in the tight space, 'How can we survive our times if we do not carry hope? Being judged on which way you might turn in a street, imprisoned for starvation or hunted, murdered even, for a certain religion and so much more. Hope carries us forward,' he laughs, as he kisses her to help disguise the fact that her question has neither been directly nor honestly replied.

Barbel joins them and takes his arm, as she passes him a fresh jug of wine,

'It is our Faith in God that will carry hope further, son. We are truly blessed and we promise to help those that we have to leave behind, in whatever way we can. Maybe, one day, it will be possible to return. I do have that hope in my heart.' Barbel brings her son's hand to her lips and kisses him tenderly, 'I am glad that you have joined us, Jowan. Let me dance with you before there is no more opportunity this afternoon.'

Jowan de Hem, for once, is unsure whether he is glad to be pulled from his situation with Greta or not. Her sadness would lend itself a further opportunity of a warm and intimate goodbye, but her neediness is tricky and he soon settles his conscience that it is better left as it is. Looking over to his father, he sees that he is immersed in conversation with Greta's father, Joos Van Brake. He knows the old friends will be arranging to meet, to finalise all financial arrangements.

※※※

ABOUT THE AUTHOR

Jeni was raised in the Fens and fought the endless, flat landscape that she grew up in. However, it infiltrated deep into her bones. She only recently came to appreciate its effect and the creativity that can come from living somewhere so lonely and vast; where sky becomes land, and the sea is never far.

Thanks to Norwich City Council providing affordable adult classes in creative writing, and a sense that it was 'the right time', Jeni began to write with flourish a few years ago. When she discovered her pen name, Jeni Neill, it seemed as if it had been waiting for her.

She would urge anyone with the nag of an idea, to set it down and begin the process of writing:

'It gives a freedom I have never really known before; it gives a voice. To be heard and understood is a pretty fundamental human need. Lots of things can block this, but writing can free it.'

If you would like to follow Jeni on social media, please visit her blog:
https://jenineillauthor.com
Instagram: jenineillauthor

Online reviews are most welcome, if you would like to recommend this book to others.

ACKNOWLEDGMENTS

My foremost thank you must be to my father, John Hall, who brought my mother to the Fens, where they then took root to raise their family. If I hadn't been fed by that landscape and chosen the fen roads which I did, would I now be writing as I do? But, my father has also been enthusiastic and most supportive of this collection of stories; eager to read the next one, often before I was quite ready to send it! His critique and impressions have been most helpful and the bond created between us, over the regard of acres of flat, unassuming land, has been both vastly unexpected and valuable, in equal measure. Thank you too, for letting me use your painting 'Fen Road', which was born many years before I would have considered my own connection to it.

Thank you for your editing, Alexandra. I'm not sure that a writer is supposed to get so excited about receiving annotations, but I do with yours. Your enthusiasm is contagious and thoughtful considerations integral to the finished work.

Thank you for your proof reading, Kirsty. I eagerly await your improvements too, and they come back so efficiently that I really marvel at how you balance the demands on your time.

Thank you to Mark and Sarah at Dynamic Print. It was just as enjoyable working with you this time, as it was with The Devil's Dye. Mark, you soothe my stress brain with your professional ability to create a cover, bringing all the exacting measurements and elements into line.

Vellum was used for formatting, a commendable software programme. It has, like Biddles Books and KDP, made self-publishing possible, and so I am immensely grateful to these businesses for that. Nigel at Biddles Books was an excellent discovery and found, like most threads in my creative process, fortuitously and therefore seemingly meant to be. That his business is based locally in Kings Lynn, only added to this sense of fate.

Thank you to my husband and boys for sharing your time with me, with a screen. I didn't steal away for such contin-uous and prolonged stretches of time with this book, as its rhythm is different and construction more segmented than its predecessor's intensive chunk, but you have all been most generous with the portions that I have needed to take.

Lastly, please can I thank you, the readers. It is an amazing honour to sell just one book. Out of all of the millions of books to choose from, and the multiple demands on all of our time, it is quite something to have just one person spend some of their time reading this book. Thank you. It is much appreciated.